At precisely six o'clock in the morning, he stood at attention in front of what was known as the East Door of Action Mountain. From the outside, the portal was completely camouflaged, hidden by foliage and accessible only by Weston and Captain Action himself.

He watched as the immense steel door's flywheel spun and a series of inner locks clanked and clunked. Then the door opened inwardly and a blast of fresh air hit him.

The rising sun flared in through the doorway and he pulled his cap down a bit and raised a hand to shield his eyes. A silhouetted figure stepped into view, the smell of cigar smoke following it.

"General, good morning," said Drake saluting. "Thank you for putting this together so quickly."

The bright sun ushered in another figure. Captain Action stepped forward, held out a hand.

"Welcome to what we call Action Mountain, Sir. I…"

He stopped dead in his tracks. The figure before him coalesced into solidity. He saw a hand reach up and remove a blindfold, revealing a beautiful woman.

"Ahem. Here's your expert, Captain," mumbled the general.

Captain Action-Riddle of the Glowing Men
Story © 2012 Jim Beard

Published by Airship 27 Productions
www.airship27.com
www.airship27hangar.com

Interior llustrations © 2012 Rob Davis
Cover illustration © 2012 Nick Runge

Editor: Ron Fortier
Associate Editor: Becky Beard
Production and design by Rob Davis.

ISBN-13: 978-0615671383
ISBN-10: 0615671381

Printed in the United States of America

10 9 8 7 6 5 4 3 2 1

AIRSHIP 27 PRODUCTIONS

/
TARGET

Some days he just wasn't himself.

As he flattened himself against the wall, poised to spring, ready for action, he smiled at the thought. Here was one of those times when one mission had barely seen completion before another emergency reared its head and called for his attention: dangerous intruders in the building… evacuation…but one lab still occupied and its occupants unreachable.

So he put on another one of his many hats and took on the task. There were no second thoughts about it for him.

He'd asked to be sent in alone. It made sense, he'd reasoned with his superiors; he was the best-equipped to slip in and slip out again, after securing the lab workers who'd been too deep into an experiment to realize an evacuation had been set in motion. Arguments were presented, counter-arguments were counter-presented.

In the end, he went in alone. Better a scalpel than a hatchet.

One of the arguments made was that, upon their arrival, the intruders had specifically asked for him. With that in mind, he promised he'd keep a low profile.

Up ahead, the corridor turned to the right. He noted orphaned carts and other sundry evidence of the swift evacuation. He paused, making a pancake of himself against a wall next to a fire extinguisher, listening for his stalkers.

Yes, the hunter had become the hunted, a turn of events not at all to his liking.

He'd found the two men not five minutes into his reconnoitering of the building. They were crossing – shambling, almost - through a lobby when he'd come around a corner. He called out for them to drop their weapons, to hit the dirt – they replied by shouting at him in loud, coarse voices, inarticulate sounds that echoed through the empty lobby. Something flashed in the raised hand of one of them.

5

In his hand he carried a tool of amazing properties, an electronic pistol, smaller and more compact than the electronic rifle he'd used before. The weapon discharged a string of electricity – 100,000 volts – along a stream of ionized gas. It was enough to bring a charging ox to its knees. The downside was that it only carried three charges and made something of a racket when he charged it up before each shot.

He fired once, twice. The men simply disappeared into the darkness, as if they weren't even there at all. If he'd hit them, there was nothing left behind to confirm it. He never even got a good look at them.

Somehow the intruders had turned the tables on him. He never went into any situation cocksure, assuming he'd conquer and be done with it; that led to carelessness, and carelessness too often led to accidents. But, on this occasion, he'd somehow allowed his prey to double-back on him and put him at a disadvantage.

Suffice to say, it wasn't a good feeling. The building was immense, designed more like an ancient labyrinth than a modern organization's headquarters, or so he'd always thought. Even his superiors got lost in it, on occasion.

He suddenly remembered something that a good friend of his, a professional game hunter, had once told him—when the hunter finds himself following his own tracks, it's time to get out of the jungle.

That cheery *bon mot* made him think about his friend…and his friend's death…and the boy…

No time at the present for that. He shook off his reverie.

Approaching the building's commissary, he oriented himself. He stopped and listened again, thought he could hear noises in the kitchen area. He checked his pistol, made sure he still had the last charge its designers promised. Slipping through the swinging door into the kitchen, he walked silently across the area and crouched down behind an industrial-size stove on the far end.

Only thirty seconds had passed before he heard a shuffling sound in the corridor outside. Suddenly the lights flickered. Once, twice…then sputtered as if fed by a surge of electricity. Then died.

He wondered at that, but forced his attention back to the door. Someone was near, on the other side of it. An odor came to his nose, one of must and mothballs.

His eyes were then drawn to the bottom of the door. Light, but not the building lighting. In the pervasive darkness of the kitchen, a soft illumination slid up to the door from the hallway and spread out there.

He hefted his automatic, flexed his finger over the trigger.

A burst of light nearly blinded him. The regular overhead lighting had snapped on, but far more intense than at its normal level. Stars danced before his eyes. Then darkness again. Total, inky darkness. He wished he had his infra-red goggles with him. Then, voices. At first it was seemingly nonsense syllables, but he discerned a rhythm in it, a language of some sort – he was sure of it. The words came haltingly; initially slow, they increased as the conversation continued. The voices were cold, devoid of any warmth.

He could have sworn that, within what he guessed to be language, some of the words were Russian.

Then he heard his own name mentioned.

The need, the heady desire for action, not *waiting*, coursed through him. It had always been his weakness, the urge to act, and only his keen mind and decisive intelligence kept him from acting rashly. He'd seen too many good men and women throw their lives away to rash action.

But he needed to turn the situation around, in his favor, and see innocent people to safety. He'd seen the bodies of the guards the two men had killed as they made their way into the building; there'd be no more of that, not while he was present and able to act.

The voices stopped, the strange light receded, and a shuffling sound could be heard trailing away from the door.

He jumped up and made his way to the door. Listening at it for a moment and hearing nothing, he reached out and slowly swung the door in towards himself. Then he stepped out into the corridor, his sidearm humming loudly as it charged.

A heavy fist came crashing down on the back of his head. Then another blow, this time to his temple. He fell against the wall, jarring his shoulder. Somehow he hung onto his gun.

He turned towards his attacker and fired. The sharp flash of the electronic pistol slashed at his eyes in the darkened corridor, and the boom of its release deafened him. The lights flickered like lightning overhead and then stayed on. A body lay at his feet. He swiveled around to look down the hall at the other intruder.

He had never, in all his extensive travels, seen anyone dressed like the man. He wore a thick black suit that appeared to be more then ten years out of date, maybe more. It was wrinkled and ill-fitting, tight in some places, torn in others, and hanging off the man in still more. Strangely,

He swiveled around to look down the hall at the other intruder.

there was no shirt to be seen beneath the suit coat, but what looked like loops of soft animal hide hung around the man's neck. His skin was chalky white, almost sickly-looking, with a reddish aura around his facial features, the hollow of his throat, and around the knuckles and nails of his long fingers. His hair was dusky brown, not long, but shorn in a crude, lop-sided fashion.

On his feet the man wore some sort of deerskin footgear. His pants bunched up to reveal leggings of similar construction. Around his waist, cinched tightly, the man sported what looked like a short apron. Or it may have been a decoration, for pictograms of a fashion were stitched into the material. The apron was fringed, but the fringe was falling off in places; the man had apparently been sleeping in it. In fact, overall it looked like he'd been sleeping in the entire ensemble.

The strange apparition peered out at him through sunken eyes, blinked ,and shook his head almost imperceptibly. A questioning expression washed over the man's face, spreading into full-blown confusion.

Then, madness.

He watched as the man raised his long fingers to his head and suddenly seized it in a tight clamping action, rocking it from side to side and squeezing his eyes shut. It looked like nothing less than that the intruder was at heavy odds with himself.

Fighting with himself.

He could sense the inner turmoil from where he was standing. Then, a sickly feeling crept into his belly and took root there. His head swam; he felt his face flush, too. He suddenly wanted nothing more than to back away from the stranger and move far off from him.

The lights abruptly flickered and hissed, snapping on and off, bathing the entire corridor in a weird strobing aura.

Finally they shut off all together. And, in the sudden all-encompassing darkness, the man *glowed.*

The sick feeling of nausea was enough to make him want to drop to his knees. He tried to raise his gun at the weirdly-illuminated figure, but it was all he could do not to let it slip from his grip and to the floor.

The man's skin seemed to glow from within, not from any epidermal effect. It was not bright, this light, but it was enough to illuminate the man's presence in the corridor. It was enough to make him a target.

He brought his pistol up and took aim. Then he remembered every last charge in it was already spent.

The glowing man howled. A plaintive, haunting sound, it echoed through the corridor. And, like before in the lobby, he was gone in the wink of an eye.

The sensation of illness subsided then, and he gathered his wits about him. Cloaked in an odd sense of security that stemmed from the intruder's departure, he glanced once, quickly, at the prone figure of the other man, the one he'd shot. A dull, sickly light came from the stranger's exposed skin, but he could see it rapidly diminishing.

He prodded the man with his boot and, satisfied that he was dead, sprinted off down the hallway in the direction of the lab – the lab that held people who most likely hadn't a clue as to what was going on in the building.

Finding the access door to the area, he paused in front of it and looked down at the security panel set into the wall there. He punched in a memorized code and waited while the system acknowledged it and unlocked the door. With a slight hiss, it popped open about an inch, and he grasped the handle and flung it open. *So far so good*, he mused.

The door opened into an antechamber just outside the main bulk of the laboratory. He jumped over to the door on the far side of the room and moved swiftly through it. His thoughts were centered upon the glowing man – he could be anywhere in the building, even heading towards the lab for all he knew.

Two sets of eyes met his. Two female lab workers in the middle of their work looked up at him in alarm. One gasped.

"Doctor Montford!" she cried. "What are *you* doing here?"

That stopped him in his tracks. He reached up to touch his bearded chin, forgetting for a moment that he wore another man's face. He smiled crookedly and shook his head, almost ashamed at himself.

Some days he buried himself in a role.

"No, no – Janine, it's me," he said quickly. His fingers reached out to pull aside his tie, rip open the white dress shirt he wore. Underneath, the girls could see a deep royal blue uniform adorned with a dynamic symbol, a colorful triangle of arrows surrounding the stylized letters "CA."

"Oh!" said the girl, a relieved smile spreading over her pretty features. "Captain Action!"

Some days that was him, too.

He looked at Janine, a long-legged brunette he'd always intended to ask out, and then over to her lab partner, a bespectacled young woman with sandy hair and a studious countenance.

"No time to explain. Intruders in the building. Time to leave."

He held out both hands. "C'mon. Let's go."

Miles Benson Drake was, quite simply, the A.C.T.I.O.N. Directorate's finest operative. He'd risen through the ranks of its agents to become, literally, a living, breathing manifestation of the organization's acronym, a champion whose feats and accomplishments had earned him the code name "Captain Action." Drake had also become the Directorate's face to the outside world. Using his real face, of course.

A.C.T.I.O.N. stood for "Advanced Command for Telluric Interdiction Observation and Nullification." The autonomous organization, empowered by a secretive arm of the federal government, claimed to be protecting the planet from the threat of alien invasion; its existence had been public knowledge for roughly a year, after working for the better part of a decade under a cloak of secrecy.

All the better to stem the burgeoning tide of bug-eyed monsters, perhaps, though the average man on the street, if quizzed, probably had no real idea what the Directorate actually did. Though that average man did relish hearing of the adventures of its top agent.

Captain Action moved like lightning through the corridors of A.C.T.I.O.N.'s headquarters, with two young ladies in tow and a mind to move them expeditiously to a place of safety. At each intersection and at each corner, he silently motioned them to get behind him and wait for his all clear. In this fashion they made good time, and the weird apparition of the glowing man did not reappear.

Finally outside and into the waiting arms of the Directorate's security force, he released his charges to one of the organization's true doctors. Stepping off to one side of the outer courtyard, he scanned the ranks of the security men in their body armor and helmets and watched as they marched up to the building to either neutralize the remaining trespasser or confirm his retreat.

Drake let out a breath he hadn't realized he'd been holding and dug his fingers into one cheek. He pulled at it, and, stretching with his grasp, the skin tore away after a moment.

Plastiderm was one of the prizes the A.C.T.I.O.N. Directorate had secured in their ongoing struggle against alien encroachment. The foundations of the amazing material, an almost *living* clay, sprung from captured alien technology and formulated into one of Captain Action's greatest tools in his missions against the enemy.

Miles Drake was an incredible natural mimic, even as a child, and plastiderm had allowed him to advance his chameleonic abilities to the nth degree. Once sculpted and formed, it could be worn as a tight, formfitting mask, and, in doing so, the wearer could be easily mistaken for someone else.

In the hands of Captain Action, it became the key to a million masquerades. Coupled with Drake's gift for acting and nuance, plastiderm meant the possibility of replacing anyone on the planet with an exact, undetectable double...himself.

Pulling the last shreds of his temporary role as Doctor Paulus Montford - a Directorate physician formally under direct threat from organized crime - from his face, the captain balled them up in his hands. The face of the glowing man floated through his thoughts.

It was the damnedest thing. Little of it made sense.

"Captain – report."

Drake glanced up to see the approach of a uniformed man seemingly carved from a slab of granite and with a face to match.

"Building's cleared of employees," Captain Action told Major General Harlan James Weston, head of the A.C.T.I.O.N. Directorate. "I got *one* of the intruders, Harl. But the other...not sure what to tell you there. Gone. Poof. Like he was never there in the first place. I can't explain it."

"Ready to go back in?" Weston asked, though the timbre of his voice indicated more command than question. "Leading a cleanup squad?"

Drake straightened, saluted snappily. "Yessir, Sir," he snapped off, smiling, though his attention drifted to the young ladies he'd just rescued.

The general noticed and chomped down hard on a grin. "Ten-*shun*, Captain! Back into action, Miles...business before pleasure."

// MOUNTAIN

With the setting sun all but filling his windshield, Captain Action settled into the cushioned seat of his vehicle. He increased his speed, trying to clear his mind and let the stress of the day flow off him. The wind tore at his head and shoulders; in a curious way, it relaxed him.

In the droning rush of air, he mulled over the direct order given him by General Weston only thirty minutes before: Go home.

The captain had gone back into Directorate Headquarters alongside A.C.T.I.O.N. troops after its invasion, and hours later they'd been able to proclaim the entire building secure. After that, he'd been checked out by a doctor and even scanned for radiation exposure. Clean bill of health all around

Those tasks completed, he'd turned to Weston to tell him he'd head over to the security wing to examine the intruder he'd taken out. The general was swift and succinct in his response: No.

Miles Drake protested. The general chomped down on his cigar, frowned. He then informed his top-agent that since the man was still unconscious from the electronic pistol, there arose an opportunity for Captain Action to be debriefed on his previous mission and then to get some shut-eye. No ifs, ands, or buts about it.

As a former Navy SEAL, Drake completely understood the chain of command. He also understood his own body and his ability to compartmentalize stress and strain. He'd slipped quickly from one mission to the next many times before and always remained at peak proficiency, so he didn't see the problem. But, in addition to being his friend, Harlan Weston was also his commanding officer, and an order was an order.

Captain Action, though, itched to be there when the Directorate bogeymen interrogated the prisoner.

Piling on the speed, he headed towards home, mildly chagrined. "Home" being what some in the organization referred to as Action Mountain.

Drake thought of his mountain complex as a haven, a retreat, one of the perks of nearly killing himself to be the best and brightest of all A.C.T.I.O.N. agents. Originally a series of caves set in the side of a mountain in a range that lay several miles from Directorate headquarters, he'd moved in and worked with Directorate engineers to convert it to his own personal base. Now Action Mountain housed not only a laboratory, a machine shop, and a disguise warehouse, but also living quarters.

Traveling the interstate for a few miles he exited onto a little-used side road just as the last vestiges of day gave way to night. Now surrounded by mountains, he turned off the road onto a dirt path, kicking up a cloud of dust with his wheels. After a few hundred yards, Captain Action flipped on headlights and burst out onto another road – a private road.

Then he really opened it up.

The Silver Streak defied every convention of motor vehicles. More a combination of airplane and watercraft than a true automobile, the unique "whatsit" easily conquered any type of terrain the captain could throw at it.

Tri-wheeled, the vehicle boasted powerful dual jet turbines and ultramodern detection and security systems – Miles Drake often joked that the Silver Streak could probably operate entirely on its own, given the chance.

The private road he traveled wound around Action Mountain and to what Drake thought of as the "back side." There, the paved path led to the massive doors of the complex's garage, the entrance to his sanctuary, far from the prying eyes and ears of the public. Captain Action was as gregarious as the next man, but he did occasionally look forward to the seclusion the remote outpost provided him. When not jumping around the globe, he worked on much of the gear he used in the field there, tinkering and puttering with every piece of equipment the Directorate boys could dream up.

Far from the interstate and on his own turf, the captain allowed the Silver Streak to really show what it could do. The great curve around the mountain eventually straightened out and he goosed the amazing vehicle down the last treelined stretch. A young man of his acquaintance insisted on calling it the Dragstrip.

Smiling at that, Captain Action's eyes darted to a switch on the dash. He toggled it, activating a unique instrument on the Silver Streak's protruding nose, an "electric eye" mechanism, completely invisible but capable of opening the immense steel doors of the garage at the end of the Dragstrip. He guessed he was just about in range for the beam, according to the radar scope set into his dash.

The scope abruptly flickered and died.

Drake tore his eyes back to the road, alarmed to see a dark figure step out from the brush and directly into his path.

He hit the brakes, cranking the wheel and jinking the Silver Streak to one side.

A series of valves automatically reduced hydraulic pressure to the rear brakes. That allowed him to retain traction and steering, but such a swift, violent action, coupled with a forceful swerve, sent the vehicle rocketing off the narrow road.

In one split second Captain Action saw the man, glimpsed the trees, and then...nothing.

He opened his eyes to find himself still held fast in the seat safety webbing. Silently acknowledging that his finely honed reflexes had saved his life, Drake suddenly smelled smoke and quickly unlatched the belts that held him down.

Seconds later, the Silver Streak's fire suppression system kicked in and dampened the fiery heat pouring off the still-whining turbines. He lifted himself from the cockpit to step out onto the nose of his vehicle, only to realize it no longer possessed such a feature.

A tree, ancient and thick, had replaced the front end of the vehicle. It and the Silver Streak were now one.

Somewhat dazed, Captain Action peered out into the darkness, trying to make sense of what had just occurred. Had he really seen a person on the road?

Reaching back into the cockpit and into a small locker set under the dash, he removed a .45 revolver.

Drake set his back against the wrecked vehicle and checked the weapon, verifying the full clip of ammunition. He'd rather have had the electronic pistol, but it had been left behind at Directorate HQ. As Captain Action, he was loathe to use lethal force if it could be avoided but also felt the immediate situation demanded he be armed.

Something else was wrong. Drake reached up to his forehead and found it sticky and wet. His fingertips revealed the reason: blood. His own. But there was something else...

His hat. His hat was gone.

The captain looked all around him. The hat had become a part of him in recent years, something he'd found by accident on a mission and adopted as part of his specialized A.C.T.I.O.N. uniform. A silly affectation, perhaps, to wear a yachtsman's-style cap on top of his modern protective outfit, but it had become his symbol. The symbol of Captain Action.

He stepped gingerly towards the back of the Silver Streak, wary of the heat still oozing from its engines and favoring an unresponsive ankle that was beginning to concern him. There, though the sun had set and obscured the landscape, he spied his hat. A bit of remaining light twinkled off its silver anchor emblem.

Then he saw a pair of dark legs walk into view and a sickly-glowing hand reach down and grasp the hat.

He immediately assumed a defensive posture. Senses heightened, Captain Action holstered his sidearm and tamped down his natural inclination to wade right in with a blistering attack; he *had* to find out what the strange figure wanted…what it represented.

The glowing man held up the hat, looked at it queerly. His sunken eyes then floated from it to its owner. The captain could see recognition blossoming in the illuminated orbs.

The man whipped the hat to the ground, savagely, and lunged at Drake.

Captain Action clapped his hands together in front of himself, as if praying, and drew them apart to break the two-handed grasping of his opponent. Then, quick as a wink, he drove a knee up into the man's jaw. The loud sound of bone against bone echoed in the evening air. The man's head snapped back violently, but he kept his feet, only staggered.

The strange man shook his head, flopping it from side to side, then lunged once again for the captain. Drake ducked once, twice in succession, expertly avoiding his foe's grasp. On the third attempt, he drove a fist into the man's skull, knocking him backwards and to the edge of the paved road.

"Stay down!" barked Captain Action. "Let's try to figure this out without fighting! Maybe you just need help…"

Ignoring him, the glowing man scrambled to his feet and ran directly at Drake; so swift was the action that it caught the captain off guard and the two men went down hard in a tangle of limbs.

Practically growling, his opponent got his hands around the captain's neck over his high collar. Pale, bony fingers tightened – the pressure was intense. Drake was stunned by the man's strength, belying his seemingly sickly, befuddled appearance. His oxygen disappearing rapidly, he began to lose his own strength under the assault.

The man was very efficiently choking him to death.

Whispering came to Captain Action's ears, a sibilant, hissing trail of words he could barely make out. Then he realized it was coming from the glowing man who was choking him.

The captain struggled against the unbearable pressure on his windpipe. With it cutting off his oxygen, he wasn't sure how much longer he had until unconsciousness and then…

Bizarrely, he focused on the words that drifted from his attacker's mouth, a string of syllables that he grasped at, but that remained elusive. There *was* Russian mixed in with…something else. If only he could breathe, manage to draw in even a tiny bit of oxygen to fuel his rapidly-shrinking thoughts - but the glowing man maintained his inhuman pressure.

"*Zlo…zloy…zlo…*" the man hissed. Captain Action could scarcely believe his ears.

He dug his fingers into the man's hands, searched for pressure points, some way to lever loose his insane death grip.

"*Zloy…zlo…zlo…*""

Grasping at straws, the captain tried to imitate the man's speech. Despite hovering at the brink of death, he reached out and grasped at something, anything, he might use to still his attacker's violent mission. Incredibly, and though he could only speak Russian in imitation of the man's hodgepodge talk, he mimicked the tone and timbre well enough.

"*Poz—pozvol'te mne perejti…*" he whispered through dry, parched lips. *Let me go.*

The man cocked his head to one side, as if listening to something mundane, like a bird or a radio playing somewhere. His eyes revolved in their sockets, but came back to stare down at him.

The pressure on his throat did not lessen.

Drake, gasping for air, looked up at the pale, internally illuminated face of the man; drawn and stretched over his skull, it almost appeared as a mask. The man was looking back at him, but there wasn't any focus behind his eyes. As he'd witnessed back at Directorate HQ, it was almost as if he wasn't really there…as if someone else was directing the show.

Drake forced his last bit of strength into a blow aimed at the man's head. It was like hitting a boulder. Spots appeared before his eyes. The night crept in, closer, closer…

"Cap!"

There was a sizzling crackle, a bright burst of light and then the smell of something burning. The man shook, bucked his body, flung back his head, then let it drop. His grip on Captain Action's throat relaxed. A line of spittle dribbled over his lips and his eyes rolled up in his glowing head.

The captain shoved his attacker off him, his oxygen-starved body gasping for air. The man's scarecrow form fell over onto the edge of the road with a soft thud.

"Cap! Cap! Are you okay?"

Miles Drake rubbed his neck, and then with a swift jerk, cracked it. He sat up, woozy. Trying to focus his vision, he saw a figure trotting up to him.

A boy, a young teenager, carrying a wild-looking white rifle.

"Did I do that right?" asked Sean Barrett, a tremor in his voice with a heightened note of excitement behind it. "You gonna be okay?"

The kid looked down at the still, sprawled form of the glowing man. "What a weirdo."

Captain Action Stood and dusted himself off. He held out a hand to the boy, motioning for the rifle.

"Better let me take that, Sean."

Sean Barrett handed over the weapon, his eyes still lingering on the glowing man. He crossed his arms and then took his chin in one hand, an incongruous gesture for a child his age.

The captain clicked on the still-charged electronic rifle's safety, then scanned the surrounding terrain.

"Thank you, Sean," he said finally, clasping the kid on the shoulder. "That was a close one."

He had rescued the boy from dire peril in a compound in Argentina only a month before. The pain from the event was still fresh, for both of them, but perhaps the boy was hiding it better than he himself was. Sean Barrett had lost both his parents in a heinous act of treachery and murder and Miles Drake had taken him in until he could figure out exactly what was best for the boy's future.

Bryce and Kathyrn Barrett had been dear friends. Their deaths still haunted him.

Sean had put a bright face on it, remarkably, and looked up to Captain Action as his hero and, yes, even a surrogate father. Drake had to admit that the kid, a handsome, rough-and-tumble adventurous spirit, was adapting to his new life with far more patience then he'd ever expected. And he was actually fun to have around. Most times.

"Hold this again, please," instructed the captain, holding out the rifle for Sean to take. "We've got to get this guy inside."

"Aww, I say we just leave 'im out here, Cap…" The thirteen-year-old toed the man's arm, let it flop back down. "He was tryin' to kill you!"

Drake stretched a small smile across his face, then crouched down to gather up the unconscious man to carry him. His ankle protested, but he gritted his teeth and hefted the man's body into his arms.

"Well, yes, but I need to find out where he came from and *why* he was trying to kill me. And," he cocked his head towards the mountain, "inside is the only place I can do that."

"You wrecked the Streak," pointed out the boy, peering back at the wreckage. "Now, if you can't use the Dragstrip responsibly…" He walked alongside Captain Action, towards the huge metal doors of Action Mountain's garage area, suddenly biting his lip.

"Cap, I was almost afraid I'd fry *you* with the rifle…through *him*."

"Suit's insulated," said the captain, carrying the glowing man, one wary eye out for signs of returning consciousness. "Our friend here wasn't touching my skin, just my collar. You did all right…for a kid."

Sean knew his mentor was simply teasing him. He smiled, happy to have done some good. They neared the large metal portal, the lights from inside the mountain complex suffusing the scene with warm illumination. He'd always thought the garage doors looked like giant teeth.

An alarm sounded, shattering the tranquil night air. The boy looked over at the captain, saw that he was standing just inside the doors, still holding the weird glowing guy in his arms.

"What's that for?" he shouted over the din, covering his ears with his hands.

Captain Action's face barely reflected his disappointment, but Sean could see it was there.

"Radiation," he said tersely. "It's detected radiation."

/// QUESTIONS

Almost as soon as it sounded, the alarm subsided. Captain Action looked around to see the lights of Action Mountain flicker, but stay on.

"What does that mean?" asked Sean Barrett. "*Is* there radiation?"

It was troubling; the Directorate brain-boys had cleared the intruder for spreading radiation, but the mountain base's detection system was even more sensitive. That was a necessity in his line of work, with threats from outer space being first on the list of its inherent challenges.

The captain wasn't sure what it all meant – and he wasn't going to take any chances. Hefting the glowing man in his arms, he took off across the garage area and plunged through a doorway on its far side.

"Sean – shut the garage doors behind us! The big green button!"

Ignoring the spiking pain in his ankle, Captain Action moved swiftly through the complex. As he went, he passed a computer room, armory, costume vault, communications array, living quarters, and a huge atomic generator that powered the base. Sean kept pace and kept quiet.

As they moved along, he began to tell the boy about everything that had happened at the Directorate building and up until the crash just outside the mountain. Sean listened intently; for all his exuberance, Drake acknowledged to himself what a good listener he was for his age.

Overhead the lights winked and sputtered in their wake. He thought perhaps he felt a twinge of nausea in his belly, too, but pushed it out of his mind. He dove through a doorway and into a solitary room on the opposite side of the base from the Dragstrip entrance.

Sean had never seen the area before. It looked like a tiny apartment, sparse and clean, the kind of place that maybe a college student would live in. He watched as Captain Action crouched to lay the man down on a sofa and then stood up again.

The man still gleamed, illuminating the darkness before what the boy guessed was automatic lighting coming on. Then the prone figure rattled out a wheezing breath, arched slightly up off the sofa, and fell back again.

The lights overhead flared in time with the event.

"Look!" yelped the teenager. He pointed at the man, eyes wide with question and wonder.

The captain was amazed to see the internal glow that had persisted all along begin to recede. As did the man's breathing.

"Sean, that panel there," he gestured at a nearby wall. "Behind it are a first aid kit and a small oxygen tank and mask – quick!"

Within seconds Drake had the mask over the man's face and a shot of adrenalin into his body. Finally the man's breathing evened out, but the strange glow did not return to its previous level.

He directed the boy to step outside the room back into the corridor, and, once they had both exited, the captain swung the door shut. It closed with a cold clang of metal against metal. Sean could hear hisses of air from the seals around it and the sound of some kind of clamps closing.

"Fallout shelter," explained his sponsor. "It's designed to keep out radiation. Let's hope it can keep it *in*, too. Until we know for sure about any contaminants, he stays in there and we stay out here."

Thirty minutes later, a strange setup was in operation outside the room. Captain Action had quickly assembled a cache of equipment and moved it over to the corridor just outside the fallout shelter. The boy watched as he plugged in monitors and what looked like a portable computer of some sort. The boxy apparatus was roughly five feet tall by two feet wide, with ports along its side and myriad indicators and switches.

Once it was all plugged in and powered up, the captain pulled back a large metal shutter on the wall and revealed a window into the room beyond. The glass looked to be at least four inches thick.

"Leaded glass," said Drake, rapping on the window with a knuckle. He then indicated the hastily assembled apparatus. "On this screen here I should be able to get a picture of the radiation's signature – if there is any."

Sean shuffled in place at his side, from foot to foot. "Gonna miss *Batman*," he mumbled.

The captain smiled, rolled his eyes, then sat down at a console and adjusted a few dials. The monitor in front of him popped on. A series of wavy lines appeared there, moving from left to right, twisting and undulating.

"Well, there it is," Drake whispered. The screen illustrated a radiation signature, though one he wasn't immediately familiar with. "It's radiating at a very low level, barely there from one moment to the next…might be why our boys back at HQ didn't detect it. Though I'm sure they've picked it up by now."

"Is he gonna…you know?" asked Sean, his face slightly ashen and his manner sober.

Miles Drake looked up from the monitor and at the boy. *He can't bring himself to say it,* he thought to himself. For all his courage, in spite of the brave face Sean had put on his parents' deaths, he couldn't quite say the word. Still, the captain marveled at his progress.

"I honestly don't know, Sean. I hope not. He's the only one with any answers to our questions right now."

He reached out and patted the boy on the shoulder. Sean brightened and nodded, then turned to look at the console. He *was* interested in what was happening.

A speaker on the panel suddenly crackled to life. A faint sound issued from it: a low, human moaning.

"This is a feed directly from the room," explained the captain. He increased the volume. "Look through the window and tell me what he's doing right now."

The boy scrambled to look into the room and informed Drake that the man inside was still lying there, not moving. And his glow was barely visible.

"I'm recording this," announced the captain. "I think he's talking again…"

Hours later, Captain Action sat back in a comfortable chair in his quarters at Action Mountain and tried to piece together the jigsaw puzzle of the day's events that lay before him.

After setting all the monitoring equipment to automatic, he'd destroyed his uniform in the base's incinerators. He saw no reason not to. He still could detect no radiation on his own person, but there *were* minute readings of the unique signature on his action suit.

Drake couldn't bring himself to destroy his beloved hat. He put it through multiple levels of decontamination, just to play it safe.

Then he and Sean used the mini-crane in the garage to haul the wrecked Silver Streak in for repairs. The boy was buzzing from the activity and begged him to let him stay up and monitor the fallout shelter and their guest. Drake saw no real harm in it and gave in, though reluctantly.

A spirited session of yoga and then *tai chi* eased the pain in his muscles and his ankle; the captain was relatively sure it wasn't broken, just mildly strained. He'd done worse than that while on undercover assignments and had learned to be his own doctor when the situation required he rely only on himself. Which described almost all his missions as Captain Action.

After that, Drake stood for a long while in front of the shielded glass of the observation window and pondered one of the strangest individuals he'd ever encountered.

As a child, he'd hated riddles. His parents and his teachers had seen the growing urge to action in him at an early age and a strong desire to know everything that could be known. More times than not, they simply got out of his way when he had a mind to act upon an interest or a cause – "always in motion" was what they said of Miles Drake.

But problems that appeared unsolvable, questions that seemed unanswerable…those he couldn't often bear. Oh, he soon learned the world was full of such imponderables, but, first with the SEALs and then with the A.C.T.I.O.N. Directorate, he intended to keep moving and never let such things slow him down. "Action" would be his response to everything life could throw at him.

But a strangely dressed, strange-speaking glowing man with an unknown form of radiation who tried to kill him was just about all the riddle he could stand.

The man's garments seemed to be of mixed origin. From the way he wore it, the dark, rumpled suit was quite obviously not something familiar to the man. But the leggings and the apron-like piece, those were clues to his own territory, thought Captain Action.

He'd have to do a little digging in the mountain's library; the design of the garments, the intricate stitching on the apron, he was certain resembl-ed costume artifacts he'd seen before. Eastern European? The captain knew that what he'd heard from the man during their scuffle was some kind of *mutated* Russian. The clothes didn't seem to fit exactly, but the U.S.S.R was a mighty big place, and the Soviets weren't exactly publishing encyclopedias of the native dress of every one of their indigenous peoples. Even for a master of disguise, a man knowledgeable enough to pose as hundreds of different types of citizens around the globe, he felt a bit flummoxed. Maybe even a bit out of his league. Then again, it could have been the lack of oxygen while he was being strangled.

The monitoring console abruptly let out with a soft beeping noise and Sean sprung up from dozing in a chair to wipe at his eyes and peer at the screen. Drake joined him at the controls.

"That-that means the radiation is going away, right?" asked the boy, his finger tracing the wave signature. "That might mean he's about to…"

"Yes, but he's still breathing…for now."

Drake looked at the boy, no, the young man, beside him and held his gaze. He shook off the slight feeling of dread that came creeping over him, the one that asked him why he was putting Sean in possible danger by letting him hang out at Action Mountain.

"Time to call in," he told his ward. "Let's get General Weston on the horn. This thing's gotten too big for just the two of us."

"Our man here has expired," reported Major General Weston.

Captain Action grimaced into the phone. He stood in the communications room, surrounded by several television screens, banks of consoles with blinking lights and a gigantic, illuminated map of the world.

"I was afraid of that," replied the captain. "My guest is almost there, I'd say."

"Let me get this straight," came the gruff voice through the receiver. "You're certain the one who almost killed you just a few hours ago, is the same one who got away from here earlier today? How did he know where to go? Where to find you? Why didn't he and his accomplice simply go to the mountain to start?"

Drake was silent for a moment, collecting his thoughts. He let out a breath and answered. "General, as near as I can figure, these men have been, well, *programmed*. Both there and here they showed signs of what I'd call inner resistance, as if they were struggling against a programmed set of orders of some sort. Maybe a posthypnotic suggestion. I don't think it was simply disobeying a direct verbal command such as the variety you'd give."

"It's incredible."

"I agree, but we've seen a lot of incredible things in the past few years. Look at plastiderm or some of the even wilder bits of technology we've encountered from space. Incredible as these attacks seem, I'd stake everything on another mind, another personality at play here. Someone who knows the location of Action Mountain and wants me dead."

Then it was the general's time to be silent, most likely mulling over Drake's words.

"Who all knows of the mountain base, Harl?" asked Captain Action, leaping into the silence.

"Well, beyond myself and you, of course," came the reply, "the Director-ate engineer, that's just four, and my chief of staff. But, Miles, I can vouch for every single one of them. No doubt in my mind. There's not a traitor in the bunch. And that's everyone who knows, except for the boy, naturally."

"No, there's one other, general."

A distinct coldness came over the line. Drake couldn't see the general, but he could imagine the expression that was spreading across his face.

"He's dead, Captain. You told me that yourself."

Drake turned away from the open doorway of the communications room, lowered his voice.

"No, I said I *believed* he was dead, General. When we last fought, in China, it looked like he perished when he fell from the…"

"What? Miles? What?"

Captain Action ran a hand over his mouth, stared off into the distance. "When my guest was attacking me, throttling me, he said something. I thought he was saying that I was 'bad' and I assumed he meant that as a reason to kill me. But I realize now that he was saying the word evil."

General Weston let out a whoosh of air, all at once. An icy sensation had flowed in, soaking and then freezing the connection.

"Captain," said the general, in a no-nonsense tone. "What do you need from me? This has just moved up to the highest level of priority."

"I need," Drake began, "an expert on Russia and one on radiation. I'm good, but this has taxed my knowledge base."

Weston hummed a bit, stammered. "I-I think I have just the person. Singular. For both fields, actually. Someone we just, ahh, *acquired*."

"Quite a coincidence, that," said the captain. "Okay, if you can get him out here first thing in the morning or sooner if possible."

"Miles, I…oh, never mind. I'll be there with your expert at, say," he paused, "Oh six hundred. We'll come in through the East Door."

Captain Action acknowledged and hung up. He turned to head back to monitoring his strange and enigmatic guest.

At precisely six o'clock in the morning, he stood at attention in front of what was known as the East Door of Action Mountain. From the outside, the portal was completely camouflaged, hidden by foliage and accessible only by Weston and Captain Action himself.

He watched as the immense steel door's flywheel spun and a series of inner locks clanked and clunked. Then the door opened inwardly and a blast of fresh air hit him.

The rising sun flared in through the doorway and he pulled his cap down a bit and raised a hand to shield his eyes. A silhouetted figure stepped into view, the smell of cigar smoke following it.

"General, good morning," said Drake saluting. "Thank you for putting this together so quickly."

The bright sun ushered in another figure. Captain Action stepped forward, held out a hand.

"Welcome to what we call Action Mountain, Sir. I…"

He stopped dead in his tracks. The figure before him coalesced into solidity. He saw a hand reach up and remove a blindfold, revealing a beautiful woman.

"Ahem. Here's your expert, Captain," mumbled the general.

"Ahem. Here's your expert, Captain."

IV
DEFECTOR

Liquid brown eyes appraised him, not boldly, but confidently. The eyes had an odd cast to them; origin unknown, he thought to himself.

"Captain Action," said Weston. "Meet Uliana Ulanova."

"Gold," he replied, extending his hand. "If my Russian's not too rusty..."

The woman stepped past him. "Am I here to discuss my name, Miles Benson Drake, premiere agent of the A.C.T.I.O.N. Directorate, or am I to examine your problem?"

The general jumped in. "Miss Ulanova's expertise extends to both the radiation sciences and to Russian history and sociology. She, ahh, defected to us only a few months ago."

Drake saw a woman in what he'd guessed to be her late twenties or early thirties, with a wide, pretty face, thin but exceedingly well-formed lips, and, of course, those stunning brown eyes. She wore her deep black hair short, in a gypsy shag, and her tawny skin was lightly dusted with freckles, especially across the bridge of her slightly flattened nose.

"Your English is very well," he offered mischievously.

"It is also very *good*," she replied, with only a trace of accent.

The woman turned back around and walked up to him, now reaching out with her hand. The captain grasped long, firm fingers; he resisted an urge to bend and kiss them. Interestingly, she was also somewhat cold to the touch.

"It's a real pleasure to meet you," he said, smiling.

Uliana Ulanova nodded once, curtly, then spun on her booted heel to walk farther into Action Mountain. She looked at her surroundings. Captain Action found her exotic, both earthy and excitingly intangible.

Noticing her seeming interest in his base, he glanced over at General Weston and raised an eyebrow.

"Many people don't take well to caves, Miss Ulanova," he said, observing her pleasingly "mod" outfit, a matching open-front light sweater and miniskirt worn over a mock turtleneck blouse and tights. The intriguing pattern on her sweater and skirt even extended to her boots; all together, the ensemble highlighted her generous and well-formed attributes.

"Caves do not bother me," she said distractedly. "Where is this man I have come to see, please?"

Captain Action watched closely as Uliana leaned over the monitor on the console outside the makeshift radiation chamber. She reached out with one hand and touched the screen, lingering over its visual of the strange waves of radiation emanating from his guest.

"I know this one," she whispered. Drake thought her touch upon the monitor was almost *affectionate*.

She looked up suddenly at the captain and the general and quickly pulled her hand away. "I recognize this signature, Captain. It is one that I have studied for many years now. There is no other one like it on Earth."

General Weston frowned. "Well, what's the source of it? Is it dangerous?"

"There is still much I do not know about it," Uliana responded. "But the radiation does not seem to apply itself to inanimate objects, or, if at all, at least not permanently. Only to humans. There it takes root and stays. It also has a very curious proclivity to drain energy from nearby sources.

"As to whether or not it is of any *danger*, I say only to those who carry it within them. I have never known it to radiate to others."

Weston eyes widened. "You know that sounds, well, a bit hard to swallow?"

Captain Action's eyes burrowed into Uliana's. "Let me get this straight. You're saying that there's a *source* for these people who carry this particular form of radiation? And it's somehow mutated to a stage that it remains unique to them? A part of them?"

The Russian defector stood up from her chair and stepped away from the two men. With her back to them, the captain could hear her murmuring something to herself. Then, she turned to face them again.

"Are you familiar, Captain," she began, "with what is known as the Tunguska Event?"

Captain Action caught his general's eye. A silent look passed between the two men.

"Yes, if you're referring to what's believed to be an unprecedented explosion above the ground in Siberia in 1908? Some say it was a thousand times more forceful than the atomic bomb we dropped on Hiroshima during the war. The Soviets sent a scientist, Leonid Kulik, to the region in 1930 to investigate, but he received little help from the indigenous people there. They were afraid of something they called the 'valleymen'."

Uliana frowned, nodded, her brown eyes serious and somber. "Most likely it was equal to fifteen megatons of TNT. It covered approximately 2,150 kilometers. The trees and wildlife were *decimated* throughout the entire area.

"Scientists believe it was either a meteor or a comet, plunging through the atmosphere and detonating a few miles above the ground."

Before Drake or Weston could comment, she continued. "Captain, I was a member of the Soviet Sciences Bureau, an expert in radiation. One of my assignments was the examination of a radiation wave once allegedly exclusive to the Central Siberian Plateau, a wave that exists in no other place in our country. We have spent many years determining that fact."

"How do you know it stems from that part of Siberia?"

She paused, looked down. "We had the opportunity, several years ago, to examine a male and a female who came from there, both of whom encompassed that radiation internally." Uliana then looked back up at him, pointedly. "We believe it derives from the Tunguska blast."

Shifting her eyes from the captain to Weston and then back again, she swallowed then spoke again. "I maintain contacts in the Soviet Union" She quickly held up a hand to still Drake's protest. "A fact that your government is well aware of. I have been told that an expedition, a Red Army force, has been dispatched to the area. Most likely they are aware of these men and are curious as to their origins...and motivations.

"Now," she said, stepping up close to the captain; she was almost as tall as he, able to look him directly in the eye, "may I see this man you are holding here in this mountain?"

Her exotic features, her unique scent that eluded him, played a bit of havoc on his senses. Weston nodded at him and so he turned and pulled opened the metal shutter across the window of the room beyond. Uliana stepped over to the window and looked inside.

Hanging back, Captain Action leaned into his general and addressed him quietly. He kept his eyes on the woman.

"It's all pretty strange, Harl," he said. "But in a weird way, I feel like some pieces of this *are* coming together. We've wanted to look into the Tunguska question for ages and if the Russians are heading there..."

"Just like a game of chess, these moves." Weston replied. "Speaking of which, did you hear that Fischer took the championship again?"

The two men had been rivals at chess for years, always seeking to best the other at the game. "He'll meet his match in Monte Carlo," Drake smirked. "You just watch."

"By the way, Miles," noted the general, pointing his chin at Uliana and dipping his voice even lower, "her friends call her Yu-Yu."

"Gentlemen," she said abruptly, swiveling her head around to skewer them with her eyes, "this man is dead."

Leaping over to the window and shoving the woman aside, Captain Action peered through the thick glass. Inside, the man on the sofa was completely still. His chest did not rise or fall. The oxygen mask about his face was not fogged. And he no longer glowed.

General Weston spoke up. "This scope's gone dead, too. Screen's on; no more wavy lines."

"When they die, the radiation goes with them," said Uliana, matter-of-factly. "It will be quite safe now for you to open up the door to that room."

Soon they stood over the body of the man, he who had tried to kill Captain Action several hours before. The captain pulled the oxygen mask off the man's face and gazed at his features.

"These pieces here," indicated Uliana, pointing to the man's leggings and boots, "are similar to those worn by the Evenks people of the North. The cut of the suit and the material are from, I think, Novosibirsk or even Omsk."

She looked up at the two men, almost sheepishly. "I am, err, from the Chelyabinsk area."

"And the article here, what appears a kind of apron?" asked Captain Action.

Uliana shook her head. "Unknown." Her eyes darted from man to man, then narrowed.

"Scandinavian," said Drake. "I looked into it. Oh, maybe that kind of decorative piece can be found in many regions, many cultures, but that delicate, intricate stitching? Unless I miss my guess, it's very much like Finnish work, or Lapland."

The woman paused. Her eyes widened, then closed. Her skin flushed slightly. She shook her head, but said nothing.

"Let me play you something," announced the captain. He stepped over to the console and toggled a switch, turned a dial. The speaker on the panel came to life. From it issued forth the recording he'd made of the glowing man's ramblings.

Uliana listened, seemingly deep in thought.

When it was over, she addressed Captain Action. "It is a dialect of the Central Siberian Plateau. He is saying that you are evil and must be destroyed."

Miles Drake bit his tongue. He wasn't convinced by her interpretation, but held his opinion.

"Why didn't he and his partner say any of that back at headquarters?" asked Weston. "Why weren't they as direct in their attempt at murdering you as this guy here was out on the causeway?"

"I was in disguise, remember? They didn't recognize me. They had orders. Orders to kill Captain Action, not Dr. Paulus Montford. My disguise must've caused them a lot of confusion."

"They made their way here all the way from *Siberia*?" queried the general, sounding incredulous.

The captain nodded. "Arduous, but not impossible. Probably hitched rides, stowed away on trains, in cargo containers. All because someone wanted me dead and I'm convinced that man in there didn't. He was under the overt, mental control of someone else. I'm sure of it."

He rounded on the Russian woman. "And it's not me that's evil. Or at least that's not how I read it."

"Then what?" she asked, curious. "Or whom?"

"Have you ever heard of Dr. Evil?"

The beautiful woman's face took on an odd expression, as if inwardly horrified by even the name. Drake thought she looked like she had just eaten something foul and completely disagreeable.

"No," she muttered.

"One of the worst," Weston offered. "Hitler, Mussolini, Tojo, Stalin... pikers, all of them."

"He's the textbook definition of a villain," said Captain Action. "Barely human anymore. A controller of minds, Dr. Evil looks upon everyone else as simply fodder for his experiments, foul tests in which he seeks the ultimate subjugation of the human race. I know that sounds fairly grandiose, operatic even, but to the doctor it's just a way of life. He's ruthless and cunning and intelligent beyond anyone else on the planet.

"And he personifies his name."

"He killed my parents," came a small, quiet voice from behind them.

They turned to see Sean Barrett standing there, forlorn, but with a fire in his eyes that raged far beyond his years.

"Sean," said the captain, holding out a hand to take the boy's shoulder, gently, "this is Miss Uliana Ulanova. She works for the Directorate and has come to help us with questions about our guest."

He ushered the teenager into the circle. "This is Sean Barrett, Miss

Ulanova. And what he says is true; Dr. Evil murdered his parents in Argentina. And I was too late to prevent it, something I'll regret all my days. Bryce and Kathryn Barrett were friends of mine, you see."

Uliana bent slightly at the waist and offered her hand to the boy, not as an adult to a child, but as an equal. Drake could see that Sean picked up on that immediately.

"Is he still alive?" asked the boy, turning to his mentor. "You talk about him like he was still alive."

Captain Action did not lie to children. He lied regularly as a part of his job, but he did not lie to those who it would hurt the most. He did not care to pull punches with Sean when it came to the topic at hand, though he sometimes wished he could.

"I think it's a possibility, Sean. Especially after what Miss Ulanova has told us. I think he's somewhere in the Tunguska region and sent those men to kill me. And I intend to take the fight right back to him."

"Now, hold on one minute, Captain!" bellowed General Weston. "I might have something to say about that."

"Sir, yes, Sir?"

The big man moved the cigar from one corner of his mouth to the other. He crossed his arms, grimaced. "*How*, for starters. And when?"

"ASAP," said Captain Action. "As to how, let's work that out…"

"What does it mean, 'ASAP'?" asked the woman, a confused look spreading over her face.

"As Soon As Possible," replied Sean. "This is Captain Action, ma'am. He doesn't wait for the wind to change. He's really with it."

"Don't be rude, Sean," remonstrated Drake.

Uliana took a step towards the captain, positioned herself in front of him, hands on her hips.

"Captain, I will go with you."

Drake was silent. He looked deep into her eyes; saw himself in the reflection there. A frown came upon him. But he dipped his chin and then raised it again. A single, taut nod.

"Yes, I believe you will. But you're a defector. Aren't you concerned that you're a wanted person?"

"This doctor of evil, he seems to be working with strange forces but from an area that I am familiar with. And I will be with *you*, Captain," she replied, with an enigmatic expression. "I assume you are as capable as your spies on the television, no?"

He smiled. "Yes, but not quite as handsome."

Before she could reply, Drake wheeled around to glare at Sean Barrett.

"And before *you* say it, no, you are *not* going with me. That argument's over before it's begun. You'll be heading back to the A.C.T.I.O.N. Academy after the break is over. Which is only a few days from now."

Anger flashed on the boy's face. Uliana brushed past the captain and took Sean's hands in hers.

"I have only just met you, but I can tell you are something of a 'boy wonder,' yes? Well, we have a saying in Chelyabinsk: it is better to be safe than sorry, my boy wonder. Please stay here, safe."

She turned her stare from a somewhat brightened Sean and directed it at Captain Action.

"So, we leave as soon as possible. But, as your General Weston says, how?"

"Well," said the man, rubbing his chin and looking thoughtful, "There's something I've always wanted to try."

V
EXECUTION

They brought them out at dawn and shot them. One at a time, down the line, one bullet in each of their heads while the others were made to watch.

The problem with these villagers, thought the colonel general, was that they had short memories. Every so often they had to be reminded who was in charge.

It was such a waste, he mused to himself, gazing upon the bits of blood and brain matter from the dead spattered on the bricks, and the mute, thunderstruck faces of the living. Oh, he supposed it all served to impress upon their backwoods minds the might and majesty of the Red Army, but overall, in terms of men and material, it was most definitely a waste.

The colonel general forced himself up onto his feet from his field chair and walked slowly across the little square. He stopped in front of the gaggle of villagers, just to one side of the crumpled bodies of their brethren, and, looking down upon them, cleared his throat.

"Citizens of-of...whatever the name of this village is...this execution was carried out in the name of the state, of the people and of the glorious revolution. These sociopaths", he indicated the bodies with a weak, flapping gesture, "were found to be guilty of crimes against the motherland and traitors to the state. And, so, to its people, also."

It was not exactly the truth. In fact, there was very little truth in it all. It was, for the most part, simply something to keep his men from becoming too bored.

The colonel general looked over the crowd and then above their heads to take in the countryside. *Countryside.* How he loathed even the word. He hated the outlying areas, virtually anything west of the Ural Mountains; better to stay in Moscow or Stalingrad, or even Kazan if one wanted to be so...*provincial.* For him, he wished to never see such a countryside again.

To wit, such a place birthed men and women who refused their duty to share their riches with their comrades. When they had come to this village, not far from Vanavara, they had arrived thinking that the very sight of the glorious Red Army would be enough to open any door, any larder and any storehouse. Not so in this place. The colonel general, tired from the journey over rough roads and seemingly endless hills, was told by his men that the villagers were apparently not very good communists – they had no spirit of the revolution in them to spread the wealth around.

So, a few executions were in order. To remind the lowly how to best serve their leaders. As he had once read in an English novel, "All animals are equal, but someanimals are more equal than others."

The colonel general's real name was not important. It was something to be used by his superiors for identification, nothing more. His men called him Veles, after the ancient Slavic god of the earth and of the underworld.

As a young man, quite angry, he often thought more than acted. In his deepest, innermost thoughts, he fancied himself a secret incarnation of the god Perun, the wielder of the thunder and of the lightning, the transformer. These fantasies helped him through many troubling times in his formative years. Then, when he had acquired a sufficient level of authority in his military career and wealth, he became engrossed in the study of mythology. It was then that he realized that he was actually Veles.

Veles the dark one. Veles the wronged.

The colonel general was a large figure, possessed of thick sinews of muscle, but also now with the look of a man who had begun to allow his body to lose its definition, its manly character. He had also recently taken to shaving his entire head and dispensing with facial hair altogether. So much better to show off the jagged, puckered scar that arced horizontally across his chin, a personal thunderbolt, the result of a botched attempt at sewing closed a wound.

Veles had grown somewhat soft as he became more cognizant of his divinity. He longed to walk the darkened streets of the big cities, trolling for parties, not traipse about in frosty Siberia on a fool's errand. He had become quite comfortable in being a reactionary, happier to staying put under a solid roof than languidly directing the execution of peasants in the back country. A waste of material.

Already disinterested in the execution, he looked away from the hills and turned to appraise his men. There, off to one side, were his three lieutenants, his pantheon, his dogs of war.

They too had eschewed their real names in favor of their true selves.

The tall one, with the sun-darkened skin and the sunken eyes, was known as Flins, the god of death. He did not smile, but his commander knew that his black heart danced at the sight of the spilled blood, the lifeless corpses. Veles would not be surprised to learn that the man would be found later, soaking up some of the blood with a rag for a trophy.

Standing next to him was Marowit, the god of nightmares. Thin, almost emaciated, he had the complexion of curdled milk and a personality to match. The man fingered his knives, a set of blades he carried in a special pouch strapped to his belt. Veles had only a day ago ordered the officer to curtail his hunting of the local musk deer – Marowit swore the fanged beasts possessed glands that were worth a small fortune for the smelly substance therein. Veles told him he should find a different hobby.

Apart from the other two, standing at attention with his hands clasped behind his back and a bored look floating about his face, was his lieutenant called Juthrbog by the men – god of the moon. He was an albino, with snowy white hair, icy white skin and red eyes. Even Veles found him disturbing to look upon. The man insisted he be referred to as a "scientist-soldier," but no knew exactly what he meant by it. It was said that to touch his skin was to find one's fingers instantly frozen, an experiment no one wished to conduct.

All three of the men wore a stylized lightning bolt insignia on their neat, clean, regulation Red Army uniforms that looped over their left shoulders from back to front. Colonel General Veles had strict orders that they were not to wear the symbols anywhere but in the field.

There, away from the dull, unimaginative eyes of their superiors, they were a force of nature, a law onto themselves, and the colonel general wanted them to be always reminded of that. And so, the special insignia.

His current orders had come down through the regular chain of command; no wonder that they made little sense to him.

The colonel general was to lead an investigatory thrust into the Central Siberian Plateau, to track the path, backwards, of three men who weeks before had somehow, perhaps even inadvertently, made themselves known to the Kremlin. He had seen the files on the one who was captured, now dead; Veles was forced to admit that he had never seen anything quite like the strange man. Someone, at some high level, was obviously concerned by the man and wanted very much to know why he and his comrades had walked out of the wilderness and cleverly made their way out of the country.

There were also notes of radiation, a "glow" that supposedly emanated from the men, and of the strange tongue they spoke and of their odd manner. Veles scoffed at some of it, but not in front of his superiors.

Also, in his orders, there was a rough destination: a place near the Podkamennaya Tunguska River. He recognized it as the location of the so-called Tunguska Event. He and his men were to travel to the area, determine exactly where the men had come from and, if necessary, secure anything that would be of interest to Moscow and the glorious state.

Of what exactly that would be there was no idea. But there had been far too many strange stories out of the region that had been ignored for far too long, apparently. And now this recent bit of chaos.

Veles was requisitioned two tanks, four trucks, four armored personnel carriers, and a communications vehicle. With a force one hundred men strong, he made his way to Taishet by rail and from there to the Baikal Amur Mainline junction. The entire expedition, all vehicles and all men, were put off near Ust'-Kut, and then they began their long trek northward.

With roughly four hundred miles to cover, Veles thought that they were making very poor time.

March in Siberia was not "where it was at," as he had heard the Americans say.

March meant temperatures as high as negative two-point-six degrees Centigrade or as low as negative eleven-point-eight. It did not make for the best traveling weather.

Veles had grown weary of the trees in Siberia. The region covered somewhere near ten percent of the Earth's surface, and almost every bit of it covered in *taiga* trees, the planet's largest forest.

If he had to look at one more *taiga*, he was sure he would go mad.

And communications, well, that was a joke. Something was interrupting their attempts to send a signal. Nothing seemed to be coming *in*, either, except static and small snatches of ghostly, disjointed voices.

It was surely a godforsaken place, if one believed in God, that is.

Now they had come to the little uncooperative village that did not seem to appear on any map. And they had lingered there far too long, perhaps. But, still, his orders specified no timetable for him to carry them out. So, he took his time.

Inside, though, in his deepest, innermost thoughts, the colonel general wished for a challenge. Something to test his godly powers. A Perun for his Veles.

A soldier crouched behind a scraggly bush, peering over and across the path that crossed in front of it.

Night was falling and he was cold. The cold made him a bit crazy. It seeped into him and got into his veins. He needed warmth; if he could have that he could finally sleep.

In the distance, a few of the peculiar wild horses of the area scratched at the ground around them. They dug in the soil with their hooves and then stuck their long noses into the holes, searching for roots or grubs. The soldier watched the animals, thinking of how warm they must be under their shaggy coats.

He stood up, just a little, to get a better view of the horses. The setting sun was just about gone and soon he'd no longer be able to gaze at the pathetic creatures.

But that was not why he'd chosen the spot to sit and wait.

He was soon rewarded with the sound of someone approaching. He had timed it just right; he was pleased with himself. Then he saw the girl.

She was a pretty thing, at least to his starved eyes. Under her many layers of clothing, she looked warm and comfortable. It was that warmth he desired and perhaps a bit more. It all depended upon the timing.

The soldier stood up abruptly, startling the girl. He made no overtures, no attempt at conversation. He jumped over the shrub he'd hidden behind and spun the girl around and then looped one arm about her neck, tightly. Before she could scream, he proceeded to show her his knife.

The young man had procured it from the soldier-clerk they all called Skrzak after the small, flying imps of legend. Skrzak didn't seem to care what the soldiers' intentions were for the equipment they requisitioned from him. The diminutive, myopic clerk was every soldier's friend, or so they said.

The girl's voice caught when she saw the knife that flashed in front of her face. She gulped when the soldier dragged her over to a tree and then behind it. She squirmed as he threw her roughly to the hard ground. She gasped as he used the knife to cut into her clothing, slicing it away in layers. She cried when the cold, stinging air bit into her exposed breasts and her white belly.

Then the girl whimpered when she saw the soldier begin to untie his trousers.

A light appeared out of the darkness. The girl thought perhaps it was an angel. She hoped desperately that it was an angel.

The soldier wheeled around, angry to be delayed from the warmth that was within his grasp. He threw an arm up to shield his eyes from the penetrating glare of the light. In doing so he dropped his knife and his trousers.

"What are you doing there, comrade?" came a voice from beyond the light. "Step over here. Now."

"Wh-who..?" he managed.

"*Now!* I order you to approach me!"

So terrified was the young man, so commanding was that voice, he pulled up his trousers and, holding them in one hand, walked over to the light, his other hand held out in front of him as if he were blind.

As he drew nearer to the light, he realized it was coming from the massive headlights of a vehicle.

Then he saw who was speaking to him. And he could not believe his eyes.

VI
VISIT

"**B**ut I do not understand, General Secretary," he said to the portly figure standing there in the dark, looking at him.

The General Secretary of the Communist Party of the Soviet Union balled his fists and planted them on his hips. He was a big, jowly man, dressed in a large field coat of military cut, an impressive figure despite his receding hairline, drooping jowls, and sixty-one years.

"It is not truly *for* you to understand, Colonel General," he said, as if speaking to a small child. "But I will make the attempt, regardless."

Veles had been knocked for a loop by the arrival. The ground had been summarily removed from underneath him. One of the most important men in the Soviet Union, walking into his camp, in the middle of Siberia. It strained the bounds of reality.

"I am here to personally oversee this operation," explained the general secretary, looking around him, taking in the men, the vehicles, and the equipment with his steely gaze.

"But *here*, Comrade? This is most irregular."

"Colonel General, stop and think a moment, eh? Would I have come all this way if it were not important? In fact, this mission has been deemed *too* important to the state for it to be handled by the military alone, but there is no personal offense intended, *da*?"

Veles nodded, bowed slightly. He was on unknown soil here. He knew he was to tread carefully, though he felt his anger spiking.

"This," indicated the general secretary behind him "is my personal assistant, Captain Kalla Lebedotchka. She will be traveling with me and is to record everything that is said and done."

Into the light stepped a beautiful woman, with short black hair, exotic eyes, and the uniform of a captain in the Red Army. To Veles, the woman might as well have arrived completely naked, so surreal was the entire encounter.

The colonel general wondered where his three lieutenants were at that moment. He trusted they were nearby, as they should be. While appraising her, the woman nodded once to Veles and then stood at attention by the general secretary's side.

"It is just the two of you?" asked Veles, peering into the night at the outlines of a vehicle in the distance, one from which his visitors had disembarked only minutes before.

"We two, and a driver," came the reply. "But, more to the point, Colonel General, there is to be a visit, very soon, from a foreign dignitary to Moscow. I cannot stress upon you the weight that the person carries with them, the supreme importance of the visit. I have consulted very carefully with the premier and the Council of Ministers and we have decided that there is to be no surprise whatsoever before, during, or after the visit.

"None. Whatsoever. Of any kind."

The man smiled slightly, cocked his head. "And, yes, the army, they sometimes have surprises. Accidents, even."

Now Veles bristled. General Secretary or not, he and his men were being insulted; of that he was certain.

"I feel very strongly, Comrade," he began, his face heated, his scar puckering, "that I must respectfully protest, on behalf of myself and my men. My orders…"

"Your orders, Comrade, most likely do not specify a Party escort, yes. But they also do _not_ preclude the possibility! I am the General Secretary! This is the will of the state! You _will_ obey!"

The man's heavy eyebrows shot up with his voice, which rang out in the dead night air. Then, silence. It hung heavily over the two men.

The general secretary, after standing and staring at the general for a moment, affixed a smile to his face and stepped closer to Veles.

"You are known to us," he enunciated very clearly and very quietly, leaning in towards the general in conspiratorial fashion.

Veles looked up at his leader. He knitted his brow, unsure of what was being said to him.

"A decorated hero; you have the respect of your men. But, perhaps, you are also too long without supervision? _Da_? You see yourself as a force of nature, answerable only to your own proclivities. You ornament your lieutenants in your sigil, yes, yes; I have seen it. Do not insult my intelligence, Colonel General.

"I do not wish to usurp your command here, in front of your soldiers. But the Council has spoken and my presence here has been mandated by the Party. You may even find me useful; I have been a land surveyor and metallurgical engineer in my youth. I grew up in a place much like this."

The general secretary let out a breath. It hung in the air between them, frosty and smelling slightly of vodka and lemon.

"So, I am here and here is where I am to be. I shall try to make very little noise. Please now return to your sleep. We will leave, all of us, in the morning."

He stepped back from Veles. The general nodded, saluted, and then turned to walk away.

"Oh, and Comrade?" said the general secretary to the man's back. "All executions will cease immediately. Your men are to stay apart from these villagers. Good night."

Veles directed a look at each of his lieutenants, one at a time, pointedly. They stood near his tent, in the faint glow of a flashlight.

"I don't know what exactly is happening," he said, not liking the uncertainty in his voice, "but it appears, for however long, we will be watched, Comrades."

Dark Flins beetled his brow. "Could-could this be a *trick,* a *joke* of some kind?"

"No," replied the colonel general, shaking his head. "No, it is him; I have met him before. There is no doubt in my mind of that. And I have heard many stories of high-ranking Party members appearing like wraiths at unlikely times."

He paused, collected his thoughts. Then, he looked back at the three again, each in turn.

"Go to your beds. Let your mortal forms rest, but allow your true beings to roam."

Far off from the village and the army encampment, on a low hill, a dark shape sat. It looked over the vehicles, the tents and the soldiers.

Snow had begun to fall while the figure crouched and observed. At first a few flakes, and then a steady curtain of it descended. The wind blew and the air grew colder.

The figure then stood. Turning its back from the encampment, it clicked on a small light and shone it on a small spot on its sleeve. Silvery material could be seen momentarily, but then the light was extinguished. The dark shape moved away from the village and the soldiers, walking down the

"It appears, for however long, we will be watched, Comrades."

opposite side of the hill that faced them.

Unknown to the watcher, on another hill nearby, a somewhat taller one, four shadowy figures stood. They gazed at both the encampment and the dark figure that watched it. They conversed briefly with each other in low tones. Upon arriving at what seemed to be mutual agreement, they melted into the dark recesses between the *taiga* trees and were gone like phantoms.

Sleep eluded Captain Lebedotchka. She rose from her makeshift bed and slipped out into the biting cold of Siberia, looking about her as she did. Not wanting to disturb her traveling companion, she moved about quietly.

Outside in the darkness, she leaned up against the immense armored vehicle she'd just exited. Far larger than the BTR-152 personnel carriers of the expedition, it appeared modified, perhaps a newer advancement on its smaller cousins.

The captain rubbed her ungloved hands over her cheeks, then loosened the collar of her heavy jacket. Reaching into a pocket, she took out a small vial, removed its cap, and let two capsules spill from it and into her hand. Staring at them for a brief moment, she then swallowed the capsules.

The woman set her head back against the carrier's side, exposing her throat. Rubbing her stomach, she grimaced, as if a wave of nausea swept over her. She breathed deeply, in and out, then walked towards the rear of the vehicle.

A wolf cried out, somewhere far off, and the captain smiled. She took another step in the darkness and halted abruptly, listening.

Suddenly she crouched, then sprang forward swinging one taut arm around the back end of the carrier. Her hand, flat and extended like a blade, connected with something there.

A terse, low cry. A hissed curse. Something glinted in the pale moonlight and came whisking past the captain's face, nearly intersecting with it.

She grabbed the arm connected to the knife and snapped it violently at the elbow. Then, without the slightest hesitancy, she drove one knee forward and into her attacker's midsection.

Another curse, this time louder. Hands scrabbled at her, grasped her by the neck, swung her roughly through the chilly air. Her body slammed into the armored vehicle with great force, knocking the breath from her. Her lungs burned. She saw stars.

Then a thin, homely face interjected itself into her sight, inches from her own. And there was a knife, too, sharp and deadly-looking.

Captain Lebedotchka struggled against the pressure of the man's arm across her upper body, but to no avail; despite her initial blows her assailant had the upper hand. She was pinned to the vehicle like a butterfly on a board.

Light exploded around them. She blinked, felt the pressure on her ease.

The woman looked up to see the Russian lieutenant they called Marowit, stepping back from her and sequestering his knife somewhere into his heavy coat. He came to attention at the barking voice of his commander.

"…what is going on here, but I am asking for answers!" Veles demanded. She noticed that he did not specifically address either one of them.

"Apologies, Colonel General!" said Marowit, standing like a rock, a textbook example of soldiery. "There has been a mistake. I was patrolling the area and came across the captain in the darkness, unaware that it was she. I took her for one of the villagers, looking to steal food."

Veles was nodding, obviously not taking things too seriously.

"Yes, yes, no harm done, I can see. You are to be commended for your diligence and sense of duty. Return to your tent."

The colonel general brought his attention around to the captain. "Comrade, it is not safe for you to be wandering around the encampment at night. My men are trained to deal with any suspicious behavior, yes? I must ask you to stay within your vehicle, please?"

The woman frowned, rubbed at her shoulders, still feeling the unholy pressure the man, the killer, she was sure of it, had applied to her.

"The general secretary will be informed of this, Comrade," she said, shooting daggers.

Veles nodded, bowed slightly, a queer look on his face. "As I am sure he will, Captain."

The convoy left the village the next morning. Turning onto what the locals amusingly referred to as a "road," Veles directed the collective vehicles forward, turning in his perch on top of one of the BTR-152s to see the general secretary's massive carrier bringing up the rear.

Its windshield was darkened, he noted. He could not make out its driver.

The snow had continued to fall, blanketing everything in white, including the very air. He remembered being told that precipitation was, in fact, somewhat unusual in the area, and he cursed the Sudice, the Fates of legend, for their poor timing.

The expedition traveled deeper into Siberia, heading northward.

Around them the forest seemed unending, broken only by small clearings in which the soldiers saw ravens, golden-eyed ducks, and the occasional wild boar. The air grew colder, dipping to minus twelve degrees Centigrade. The men did not complain, though they drew into themselves for warmth and wondered to themselves what sadism had brought them to this place.

Days marched on. The column stopped to bivouac every night, but the general secretary kept mostly to himself, only asking occasionally as to their progress. His personal assistant was quite often seen, whether it was making notes into her omnipresent tape recorder or perhaps conversing with Lieutenant Juthrbog.

Skirting around the minute town of Vanavara, they drove on towards the Tunguska region. Then, stumbling upon a small clutch of Evenks, the indigenous people of the area, Veles called a halt.

Juthrbog met his commander at the front of the line, speaking to him in his low, silvery manner of speech. Veles was often astounded at how much it was like conversing with the moon itself when he conferred with the albino. His lieutenant advised him that the Evenks might be able to better direct them onto a proper path into the area – and that they might even know of the three strange men who had reputedly come out of it however many months ago.

In barely any time, two of the scruffy locals were on their knees in front of Veles, with Flins covering them with a nasty-looking Kalashnikov rifle.

Through halting speech, the Evenks barely spoke proper Russian he noted with disgust, the two men told the commander that, yes, they knew of the valleymen and their sojourn out into the wider world. They knew of it, and wanted nothing to do with it.

"Valleymen," said the general with a sneer. "Is there no people on this Earth who are *not* superstitious? Very well; have them direct us to the Tunguska site."

The men refused. It was the domain of the Valleymen, they said quite plainly. And they would have no part of them or their twisted lands.

Veles looked at Flins. "Make them talk," he hissed, and then turned on his heel.

There, coming towards him then, was the general secretary and his personal assistant.

"Comrade, a word with you," said the large man. He motioned for Veles to approach him.

Slipping an arm around the colonel general's shoulders, the general secretary once again leaned into him to speak as if they were two men with a shared secret.

"I am quite certain your orders do not include the questioning of locals in such a strident manner. There is little need for it, anyway; the captain here is familiar with the area and will lead us in. Call off your man."

Veles gritted his teeth, balled one fist against his leg. The tattered shreds of his dignity, his patience, and even his honor frayed further. He turned to his Party leader and shrugged the arm off his shoulder.

"My *orders*?" he said, narrowing his cruel eyes. "Are you so familiar with my *orders*, Comrade? With all respect, I…"

"No, in fact," replied the general secretary, "I do not have copies of your orders. I thank you for bringing this to my attention. Please get them for me." He held out a hand as if to punctuate the request.

As the Americans might have said, Colonel General Veles "flipped out."

A line had been crossed, to his mind. His private world had been invaded. His dignity besmirched. His divinity sullied. He, at that moment, gave not a single damn who it was who stood before him. His face grew red with lividity.

He puffed up his chest, stared at the man. The man stared back. Neither said a word. The entire universe around them disappeared while they stared each other down.

In that moment, perhaps Veles touched upon a kind of deity, a divine sight. Regardless of its nature, the man felt a clarity of vision waft down upon him. He stared deep into the eyes of his adversary.

Then, after several long, silent moments, the spell was broken. The general once again turned on his heel and stalked off towards his personnel carrier.

The general secretary watched him go. Then he, too, turned and, with the captain in tow, made his way back to his own vehicle.

Once inside, the woman stood and allowed her comrade to stand with his back to her for a long moment, silent.

Finally, he wheeled around and glared at her.

"Well," said the man in a very different voice and in English, "he's on to us."

VII
COMMUNICATION

A shrill spike of alarm raced through Uliana Ulanova, reflecting in her deep brown eyes, on her comely features. She slumped back against her bunk inside the armored carrier.

After a moment, she composed herself by drawing the mask of Captain Lebedotchka back into place. "How? Your masquerade is exquisite..."

"Thank you," said Captain Action from underneath the layers of his role, eyes boring into hers. "I was pretty happy with it myself. But with all modesty, I don't think it's my disguise. I think I've underestimated our dear colonel general."

Undercover work was far more than simply the right clothes and a well-fashioned plastiderm mask; he knew this well from past experience. It was research and nuance and the ability to put himself into the very souls of the people he aped, but sometimes that all flew out the window in the face of a person with a particularly good sense of what was right and what was wrong in the universe.

Apparently the commander was one of those.

"I chose the general secretary to impersonate because we needed to have complete and full access to this expedition, to not be questioned in the slightest, and to be able to operate with authority and autonomy. You saw it yourself when we first arrived; they were knocked for a loop, but the fear of the Soviet system very swiftly overruled all doubts."

She held his gaze, her enticing lips barely moving as she spoke. "Can we recover from this?"

Captain Action drew himself up and tried to shake off the niggling sense of concern that threatened to chip away at his performance.

"I'll be truthful with you, Uliana. I'm not sure."

The harsh knocking of a Kalash rifle came to their ears from outside, then strident yelling followed.

The general secretary jumped towards the rear hatch of the vehicle, threw it open. His personal assistant grabbed his hand, gave it a firm squeeze.

"Please," she whispered, her eyes searching his, "be careful, Captain."

The cold air bit into his face the moment he stepped outside. *The wonders of plastiderm*, he thought to himself. So much like real skin, even to the point of allowing for real pain.

Their current encampment was in an organized uproar. He spotted Veles immediately, waving his hands at his men, barking orders. The soldiers were fitting themselves into a defensive perimeter; he could see heat rising off the barrels of some of the men's rifles.

The disguised Captain Action marched towards the general, passing through the gauntlet of his three lieutenants and pulling up next to the man. There at his side was a small, bespectacled sergeant handing Veles a pair of binoculars.

"Colonel General," he began, "what is happening?"

Veles grinned slightly, but did not turn to look at him. Already, the respect was eroding.

"We seem to have a curious onlooker, Comrade. One of my sentries spotted him on that hill over there.

"If the soldier is of any worth whatsoever, he will have hit the intruder with his first shot."

Snow continued to fall, making for poor visibility. Captain Action felt that even he would be hard-pressed to have made such a shot in the current conditions.

Veles lowered his binoculars. He appraised the disguised Drake out of the corners of his eyes, still not turning his head.

"Regardless, we are now mobilized. Please to return to your vehicle, General Secretary, I have the situation well in hand."

Suddenly three or possibly four dark figures materialized from the trees on the very same hill in question. Everyone present saw them at the same time. The little sergeant jumped back, almost as if he was going to try to hide behind his commander.

"There! There!" Veles bellowed, pointing. The air around them erupted with gunfire, loud and raucous in the cold, dead stillness of Siberia.

The general turned to the general secretary finally. "Return to your vehicle, Comrade!"

Drake was having none of it. "General," he said, low and menacing, "I will be spoken to with the respect due my…"

"*Now*," hissed Veles. "This is a military operation, Comrade, and I am its commander. A commander under orders. We are engaged with hostile targets, and I now consider us to be in enemy territory. *Your* authority is superseded by my own in such circumstances. I sincerely hope I am making myself very clear, *da?*"

Captain Action returned to his personnel carrier, frowning through the face of the General Secretary of the Communist Party of the Soviet Union. He slammed the door shut behind him.

"How bad is it?" asked Uliana. She looked pale, her bronzed skin appearing washed-out and her eyes rimmed with fatigue.

"Bad," he replied.

He wasn't about to pussyfoot around it. "We have unknowns watching us from the hills, and the Russians are aware of them. In fact, they're shooting at them. But what's worse is the general's more or less openly defying me. And beginning to enjoy it."

The captain moved across their living space and opened a hatchway on the opposite end. He stepped into an area that Uliana was not allowed in, or to even view. There had been many times over the past several days when her traveling companion had gone into the small room and shut the door, effectively closing her out.

"Why have you been so secretive about that space? What do you have in there?"

He looked up at her, his face grim.

"Insurance."

Drake stepped back from the door, holding a curious device. "And also this, of course..."

It was what the clever A.C.T.I.O.N. people called an Inter-Spacial Directional Communicator. Essentially a large metal collar with a clear dome that sat over the user's head and shoulders. Its purpose was to provide communication between the Directorate and an agent in the field. *Anywhere* in the field.

He'd told Uliana that the set worked with brainwaves, bending them into an energized impulse that rocketed out through what the scientists called the "etherical" plane. From there, the impulses were picked up by A.C.T.I.O.N. "sensitives" at headquarters and communication established.

Miles Drake thought it sounded like something out of science fiction, but, incredibly, it seemed to work.

Everywhere but in the Tunguska region of Siberia, apparently.

"You had no success with it the last time," noted Uliana, sitting down on her bunk.

"I can't just sit here and do nothing," he shot back, a bit more terse than he intended. "If we can contact Weston and update him on our progress, at least I can feel like I've done *something*."

She rubbed her eyes, felt the radiating heat on her forehead, her cheeks. "The great American wounded male ego...*not* an endangered species."

Captain Action paused in lifting the apparatus up over his head. He looked at the woman, really looked at her.

"You're ill." He did not phrase it as a question.

"Yes." No argument.

He set the communicator down, moved a bit closer to Uliana.

"I saw the pills. You only have a few left. Is it serious?"

She looked up at him and once again searched his eyes. Drake wondered what it was she hoped to find there behind them.

"It is a birth defect. You need not be concerned, Captain. I will continue to carry out my role in the mission..." She trailed off as what appeared to be a wave of pain washed over her.

"That's that," said the captain. "We're going back. Mission's FUBARed in more ways than one. I'm calling for an extraction."

"No!" She cried plaintively. Fingers like talons rushed at him, grabbing his sleeve and trying to rip the communicator from his hands.

"Uliana," he said between gritted teeth. The woman had much more strength than he'd given her credit for, especially in her condition. "Get a hold of yourself!"

Almost berserk, her nails inched closer to his plastiderm mask. If they were to get out of their situation in one piece, they'd need to preserve his role as the general secretary. They'd need to end this destructive conflict before it truly began.

So he slapped her.

Uliana fell back on the bunk, one hand snaking up to her face, holding it. The fire in her eyes, the ochre embers that had been present from the moment Captain Action had first met the woman, receded. She laid there for a moment, staring at him with no emotion, no tears.

Then she sat up. "I need to have some air," she said quietly, her words cold.

Before Miles Drake could formulate words of his own, she was out the hatch and gone.

Anger lanced through him, hot and burning. He was acting strangely around Uliana and he didn't care for it. He needed to focus on getting them both out of the area. Out of Siberia. Their lives, *her* life, depended on it.

Practically throwing the Inter-Spacial Communicator over his head and down onto his shoulders, Captain Action frowned; he had to clear his thoughts to be able to use the device properly. He flipped on the power and drew deep into himself, shutting out all the tribulations of the moment.

Still feeling the sting on his palm and fingers, he decided it was one of the hardest things he'd ever attempted. Inside the bubble of the communicator's projection array, he launched into a few breathing exercises. When he felt significantly calm, he reached out with his thoughts.

Back in the States at A.C.T.I.O.N. Directorate headquarters there was a room of psychics called "sensitives" that did nothing but convey communications from agents in the field to their superiors. Drake had little idea of how they actually operated, but, to be honest, he didn't really need to know. He just needed to know they did.

Something was blocking his thoughts this time, the signal of his etheric presence. It was almost as if he was trying to project them through barbed wire; not a complete barrier, but one that shredded his impulses and eroded his message.

Then it was as if someone threw a heavy blanket over his head.

Darkness. Frozen shadows. A deep, cold hole in the universe.

Captain Action tried to shout in his mind, but the cry came out as a muffled whimper. He fought against the darkness, strained against it, but its cold bit into him, far exceeding the discomfort from the Siberian climate outside the vehicle.

Then, evil.

He had no other word for it. No other sign to hang upon it. It desired to be called by its true name: Evil.

Drake ripped the communicator from his head, instantly shattering the connection. He dropped the apparatus to the floor, reeling from the abrupt disconnect. The walls, the bunks, the floor undulated around him.

He resisted the urge to vomit. So strong was the revulsion he felt for the…the *presence* he had brushed up against in the ether that he felt he might never fully remove its tendrils from his brain.

Worst of all, he thought he had recognized it.

The captain stored the communicator away, then looked around him. Time to figure out exactly what he was going to do. Time for action.

Instantaneous with his thoughts moving naturally to Uliana Ulanova, the rear hatch of their vehicle opened. It could only be her, he mused, for no one else other than himself could open it.

Realizing that the door remained open and no one was entering through it, Captain Action turned to see the woman standing there in the opening, snow whipping around her uniformed figure. Her eyes, her face, her entire posture reflected her playacting as a captain in the Red Army. He cocked his head and narrowed his own eyes in question.

Then, there beside her, was Veles and Flins, looking in at him.

"Colonel General," said Uliana, pointing. "This man is an imposter."

VIII

INTERROGATION

While Veles covered him with a nasty-looking Stechkin pistol, Flins jumped up next to Captain Action and cuffed him violently across the face.

"Bring him here," said the general, menacingly.

The lieutenant wrangled Drake through the hatch. He'd pulled out his own pistol and jammed it into the captive's back, digging it in with force.

Veles snaked out a hand, reaching for what he presumed to be a mask or at least heavy makeup. He hovered over the general secretary's face, looking at it from different angles, peering at it closely. Then he simply darted in and got a hold of it.

At first the plastiderm resisted, but then tore. The general, smiling in wonder, ripped the mask from temple to jaw. The material released itself from Drake's own skin, becoming subsequently loose and flabby.

"Incredible," whispered Veles. "Now, who do we have here?"

He glanced over at Uliana, but the woman would not meet his eyes. She stood to one side, hugging herself and staring at her former traveling companion.

"Remove this *costume*," hissed the general at Flins.

Soon Captain Action stood revealed. With the discarded clothes of the general secretary around him, the man allowed the Russians a good look at what he wore underneath.

Drake sported a winter version of his famous A.C.T.I.O.N. gear, entirely done up in dusky whites and grays, right down to his boots and including his well-known sigil. The suit's specially treated material seemed thin for the cold, but on closer inspection one could see it was crafted from a special quilted fabric, obviously an advancement in inclement weather protection.

"Captain Action!"

It would seem that his reputation had preceded him, even in the wilds of Siberia.

Veles' pistol drooped as he rocked in amazement at what famous fish he had reeled in. Drake noted that, then took action.

"Thank you, gentlemen," he said in Russian. "That allows me to move more freely. Much obliged."

He darted out with limbs to his immediate front and back; a curled fist to the jaw of the colonel general and his boot into the knee of Flins behind him.

Veles was staggered by the swift blow and fell backwards, dropping his Stechkin. Flins let out a small cry of pain but did not fall. Captain Action whirled around and chopped down with the edge of his hand onto the lieutenant's gun. The sidearm discharged with a loud bang as it fell away.

With another powerhouse punch, the captain drew blood from Flins' lip. Not waiting to see what other effects it may have brought on the man, he turned and ran. By then, he reasoned, the entire camp was most likely alerted to the melee.

Flins shook off the punch and moved to run after the A.C.T.I.O.N. agent, but his knee betrayed him. Almost locked in place, the joint protested the movement and the Russian toppled to the cold ground with a yelp of pain.

Captain Action sprinted away from his armored carrier and into the falling sheets of snow. He hadn't much of a thought as to where he was headed, but it felt damn good to be moving. He only wished he had his hat with him.

It was more than just an eccentric affectation at that moment: though his winter gear served to obscure his muscled figure in the current atmospheric conditions, his dark hair stuck out like a sore thumb. He might as well been wearing a target on his head.

Shouts of attention and warning nipped at his heels as he zigzagged through the encampment. At any moment he also expected to hear the dread sound of Kalashnikovs following in his wake.

He weaved in between the Russian vehicles, sometimes veering dangerously close to armed soldiers. They loomed up out of the haze of snow like phantoms, slowing his progress. He was trying to reach the edges of the camp, perhaps to then take to the hills. From there his impromptu plan faltered.

Then a kind of sixth sense, honed from countless adventures, abruptly warned him of some even greater peril. A dark shape flashed in front of him, a narrow, hairsplitting miss. Drake stopped, crouched, ready for anything.

It was Marowit.

The Russian lieutenant, gaunt and rail-thin, lashed out at his opponent with lightning moves, a thin, sharp blade in each hand like fangs or talons. The knives swished through the air, cutting across the downward path of the snowflakes and whizzing within microns of Captain Action's face and body. So quick was the man's initial attack, so savage, the captain could only respond in defense; there seemed to be no window for an attack of his own.

Time and time again, he jerked backwards to avoid the slashing blades, leapt out of the way of their steely advance. One cut made it through and he caught it with his forearm, deflecting it away from his throat. The knife slid over his uniform's special material, slicing only minutely at its surface but not penetrating.

"God of nightmares, huh?" Drake said, feigning cheerfulness. "Well, you *are* putting me to sleep."

Marowit increased his sallies, his arms nearly disappearing within the curtain of falling snow. Whereas his fellow lieutenant Flins had remained dour and stolid, Marowit's face cracked across its width with a demonic grin as he levied attack after attack on Captain Action.

Finally the A.C.T.I.O.N. agent saw his opportunity and drove a fist into the back of the Russian's left hand, the blow effectively disarming the crazed man of a blade. Drake did not hesitate for a second and swung in with a blistering left that nearly took the man's head off.

The lieutenant stumbled back a few steps, wiping at the blood seeping from his nose. He looked up at his foe with a glare that could only have come from a nightmare.

Reality rushed in. The captain suddenly became aware of his surroundings. He saw that they were fighting on the edge of the encampment, at the rear of one of the huge convoy trucks. Beyond them were hills, barely visible now through the snow and the exhalations of the two combatants.

Something glinted on one of the nearby hills. Drake saw it, tried to focus in on it.

He discerned what it was, *who* it was, in the snap of an instant.

"Dammit...no!" he swore. Then the hard butt of a Russian rifle came down on the back of his head and stars mingled with the snow.

The last thing he saw before darkness was the obscene smile of the god of nightmares.

◆ ◆ ◆

The fool on the hill witnessed the blow, saw the American agent taken down. He chided himself vehemently for exposing himself, bringing about the defeat. Panic took hold of him then. He looked all around, taking a step one way and then another, ultimately not moving from his perch atop the hill.

Moving in and becoming involved seemed to be the right thing to do. But it could also make things worse, much, much worse, and that was not an attractive option. So close to his goal, the figure wondered if it could all coming crashing down, even at this juncture.

He sat there for a very long time, thinking and trusting and hoping that Captain Action could take care of himself.

He awoke in a tent. Securely bound to a wooden chair, he looked around the tent to see Veles, his three lieutenants, the company clerk Skrzak, Uliana Ulanova, and a table that held what looked like a large battery with several cables attached to it. A series of aches and pains throughout his body told him he'd been beaten. The back of his head felt like wet oatmeal.

"I suppose," he said through blood-spattered lips, "this is the part where you tell me that none of this is necessary and I should just talk."

Veles stepped forward, hands clasped behind his back. "No, Comrade Captain; I'm afraid I must tell you that this is *very* necessary and that I and my men will most likely enjoy it very much. Oh, and of course, you should also talk."

Dread and horror crawled up to him, whispering in his ears for attention. He shook them off and tried to remember all his anti-interrogation training.

"But, Colonel General, *is* this truly necessary?" asked Uliana, moving closer to Veles and, in doing so, closer to Captain Action.

Drake caught her scent on the air. A sense of longing and of betrayal mingled like oil and water in his mind, throwing him further off-balance.

"You say that this man tricked you, Captain? That you yourself were fooled into believing he was one of our beloved party leaders? A pity. I sympathize with how you must feel, Comrade. I assume that in your organization, err, you are KGB, yes?"

The general held her in his gaze, a smug smile on his face. Uliana's face grew hot, but she said nothing. The woman simply lifted her chin ever so slightly and ignored the question. Let the man feel her answer in her unspoken derision, she thought. Let him take pride in what he thinks is a truth he's uncovered.

Veles lifted an eyebrow, but held his smile. Then he nodded once to Marowit.

Uliana gasped at how quickly the emaciated man planted himself in front of her. His claws shot out and grabbed her heavy army coat by the collar, then violently ripped it open to just below her breasts.

Before she could protest, she found her arms very securely pinned to her sides when Marowit swiftly pulled the coat down past her shoulders in one sure motion. He then pushed her down onto a small stool and returned to his original spot in the tent.

"I think," said Veles, "that you will remain very quiet, very still. For your own, ahh, protection, of course, tsarina."

The general felt Juthrbog stir next to him, most especially during Marowit's actions with the woman. Frowning a bit at that, he called the man closer and asked him to speak all that he knew about their prisoner.

"Captain Action," said the albino, slowly, liquidly. "The A.C.T.I.O.N. Directorate's most accomplished agent. Known to have involved himself in the state's business on several occasions. Wanted for crimes against our country on numerous charges. Has, until now, avoided extradition by his own government despite more than a few requests by our own.

"Also known to be a master of disguise."

Veles got his face right up into Drake's.

"If I am not mistaken, your capitalist, bourgeois 'Directorate' goes around and tells people that creatures from the outer spaces are looking to invade this planet, *da*? You fool them into believing this and then you secure their aid and somehow profit from it. You claim that you work for the good of the people of the Earth, yet you disrupt the legitimate actions of the Union of Soviet Socialist Republics when they raise the banner of truth in protest, eh?" The general rose to his full height. "It is a shame, Comrade Captain."

"He wanted only to see what it was about the Tunguska area!" interjected Uliana suddenly. "The Americans must believe there is something there of value."

"Oh, we *will* be continuing on our way there," replied the colonel general, not addressing her directly. "We are *all* curious as to what awaits us there. But first we are going to hear from the wondrous 'Captain Action' all about his A.C.T.I.O.N. Directorate and their devices; most especially the amazing second skin he wore as our beloved general secretary."

Drake smiled, chuckled under his breath.

"You find something amusing about this situation, yes?" asked Veles.

"I'm just trying to picture you in a miniskirt and go-go boots at a discotheque, General," the captain answered. "It's going to make this a lot more bearable, trust me."

The colonel general let out a sigh, then, without peeling his gaze from his captive, pointed to Juthrbog and Skrzak in turn and then the battery on the table.

"Into action, Captain Action. Let the dance begin."

He had no real concept of how long it went on.

The myopic sergeant had attached the wires from the battery to his fingers and to his neck, the whole time peering nervously out of the corners of his eyes at him. When he was finished, the little Russian nodded at Juthrbog and moved out of the way, to the back of the tent.

The god of the moon stepped forward and, without preamble, twisted a dial on a makeshift control board.

After numerous such assaults, Captain Action could barely remember the first wave of voltage.

It went on, hour after hour, question after question, trick after trick to get him to lose his sense of placement in the discussion and let slip with his tongue. He held out, somehow.

At some point, Drake recalled what a cousin of his once told him: Let it be a shock to *them* that you have nothing to say.

Night fell finally. A sweating Veles called a halt to the interrogation and told his men to get something to eat and return within thirty minutes. After standing and staring silently at his prisoner for several minutes, the big man stomped out of the tent.

The captain raised his head, it was literally all he could move, and took in the sight of Uliana, slumped on her stool, her face wet and her skin more pale than it had ever looked before.

"Tell me," he croaked. "Why did you defect?"

She snapped her face up at him, brown eyes huge and blazing. Drawing saliva into her mouth, she spat at the ground.

"Because I grew to *hate the Soviets!*"

He nodded, full of the irony, the ridiculous nature of it all.

When Miles Benson Drake was a Navy SEAL, he first heard of the A.C.T.I.O.N. Directorate. He wasn't too sure about it initially, but after learning more about the organization, he began to form a worldview that was much larger than he'd ever imagined possible. There was more "out there" than just the little blue marble of Earth; there was the potential for an entire galaxy of Earths and more. All full of life.

He thought he'd get to see some pretty strange things if he became an A.C.T.I.O.N. agent, and they seemed to want him in their ranks pretty bad. All in all, a mutually beneficial arrangement. It worked out well from the get-go.

As Captain Action, he'd seen his share of death. Fellow agents, foreign operatives he'd come to respect and admire, and, of course, a slew of enemies – every death impacted him in some way. It forced him to form a personal code of sorts early on: preserve life and if it must be taken, do so only when necessary.

Others had scoffed at his code over the years. He didn't expect anyone to understand – it suited him and he was able to fulfill his duty as an A.C.T.I.O.N. agent while upholding the code. That's all that mattered. Respect for life. All life.

Someone once asked him, "What about your own life, Captain Action? What's that mean to you?"

Drake had to admit, at that time, that he hadn't really thought about it, just as his own father probably never pondered such a thing while he was fighting Nazis in World War II. A life in the service was to be given freely for one's country, right? And if possible, make it mean something, correct?

He'd managed to slip in and out of his missions without putting too much thought to his own mortality. He figured there would come a time when the question would seem more important.

Now, at the end of a series of electrodes, Captain Action was thinking about his life and his death.

And about making it all count.

A sharp slap across his face brought him out of his reverie. *Well,* he thought, *maybe this is it.*

The captain opened his eyes to see a pretty, tear-streaked set of features directly in front of his.

"Never, ever," said the beautiful lips, "strike me again."

He promised he would never, ever again, but could he perhaps be untied?

Then someone was hugging him and then he felt his hands and feet free and the electric cables being released.

"I was able to slip out from my coat," said Uliana as she attempted to lift him from the chair he'd been bound to. "When they failed to return

"Never, ever," said the beautiful lips, "strike me again."

after thirty minutes, I got tired of waiting. And something's going on out there..."

Drake tried to focus on what the woman was saying to him, attempted to formulate the hundred or so questions he had for her, but her present safety overruled them all. Working his way through a quick, on-the-spot yoga exercise, he cracked his bones back into place and walked over to the tent door.

Almost immediately the sounds of battle fell upon his ears. He swung back around to Uliana and grabbed her by the shoulders; she winced and he quickly released her.

"The camp's under attack. Here's what we'll do..."

IX
BATTLE

A Russian soldier flew through the air and landed at their feet, his slashed throat oozing life. Lying there in the snow, he almost looked at peace somehow, despite his being quite dead.

Captain Action and Uliana dashed hand in hand across the encampment. Dark silhouettes loomed just out of reach, struggling dances of death that faded in and out of view. The Russians were being waylaid by another force, but by who or what, the captain wasn't sure.

"Keep your head down and move fast," he advised the woman.

Shouts of alarm and even war cries reached his ears, mingled with the crack of rifles and the intermittent moaning of a submachine gun. The Russian soldiers were giving voice to their fear, their outrage, and their determination to fight; their attackers seemed to be content with remaining mute.

Drake began to imagine that the figures on the hill he'd glimpsed earlier had something to do with it all.

He could only pray that the *other* figure he spotted had the sense to stay away from it.

They reached their own vehicle in short order, sidestepping the worst, most violent pockets of the growing battle. The urge to get out there and fight was almost overwhelming; he didn't hold much love in his heart for the Russians, but he didn't exactly wish to see the soldiers slaughtered like cattle. Let Veles and his lieutenants take care of themselves – their innocent subordinates, though, deserved better odds and a fairer chance at survival.

He practically threw Uliana into the back of the carrier when they reached its hatch. She yelped as he picked her up and pushed her inside, then wheeled around to glare at him. Captain Action ignored her and dived into his personal closet, scrambling to get a hold of certain items therein.

"They...they won't...most likely...kill everyone," she said weakly. "This will stop soon."

He pulled his head out from the little room and stared at her, nodding.

"You've been here before. I knew it. You wanted nothing more than to return."

"I panicked," she offered. "I…"

He stood up, strapping on a belt and pulling out what looked like headgear. "Stay here. That isn't up for debate, Comrade. Lock the hatch after I leave and *stay here.*"

One side of her mouth twitched and her eyes narrowed, but she did not argue.

"O Captain! My Captain!"

"Hey," he whispered as he opened the outside door, "just the great American wounded male ego at work."

He had to practically force his muscles to work, to move him across the ground and between the Russian vehicles. He put it down to inaction for days on end, plus the heavy disguise that had played havoc with his regular exercise routine, not to mention the effects of Russian interrogation techniques.

Captain Action then hunkered down by the front edge of one of the big trucks and took a few mental notes on the skirmish.

The attackers were human. They wore a kind of coverall made from what looked like tightly woven plant matter dyed black, flexible as cloth, and boots, leggings, and gloves of animal fur. Strapped to their torsos, thighs, and upper arms were plates of what looked to Drake like leather or some other from of dried animal hide. Helms of a burnished, dull metal sat atop their heads like skullcaps.

He was very strongly reminded of the glowing men who had tried to kill him back in the States. In fact, he was sure they were one and the same people.

And, in the fight at hand, they had it all over on the Russians.

Though he noted that the snow was lessening, the attackers used the atmosphere and the terrain to their very great advantage. They wove in and out of the men and the vehicles and moved in for kills when nigh perfect opportunities presented themselves. But the soldiers had made their mark, too; Drake saw a few of the dark men lying on the ground, the snow around them stained with blood.

Good, he thought; the soldiers were trying desperately to pull together and centralize their defense. In effect, they were "circling the wagons."

Marowit and Flins were faring much better than their fellows, he noticed. Together, the two "gods" were cutting a gory swath through the ranks of invaders, shooting and slicing them as they moved along. Oddly, Veles was nowhere to be seen.

Captain Action placed the hat he'd brought with him on his head. A white and grey version of his beloved cap, left at home, it was worn more like aviator headgear, coming down snugly over the back and sides of his head.

Ready for battle, he got up, looked around, and charged into action.

Unsheathing it from the scabbard on his belt, Captain Action wielded his unique lightning sword against the attackers. Almost two feet long, its mysterious metal and reputedly ancient construction was said to possess incredible abilities that allowed the captain to absorb and redirect energy with the jagged blade.

Frankly, he just liked its heft and thought it looked cool.

In a holster on the opposite side of his belt, he carried an electronic pistol, a larger version of the one he'd used on the glowing man in Directorate headquarters.

Drake spotted a soldier holding off one of the strange warriors with the stock of his rifle. The man was trying to knock a wicked-looking knife out of his assailant's hand. To the captain it appeared to be a miniature sickle, with a cruelly curved blade and unusual wooden grip.

He flung himself inbetween the two combatants and chopped at the knife with the pommel of his sword. The dark figure grunted in pain and dropped his weapon. Drake then put him down with a powerful uppercut to the jaw and followed up with a charge from his pistol.

Behind him the soldier muttered his feeble thanks in Russian, apparently completely bewildered by what had just transpired.

Captain Action moved on, flitting like a phantom in and out of the fracas, coming in low and using the valleymen's ghostly tactics against them. He was sure now he knew the source of the local legend; the valleymen were all too real – and quite deadly.

To the eyes of the soldiers, they saw what they thought was a ghost, a whirling dervish of a fighting machine that sent invaders sprawling and saved the lives of more than a few of their comrades.

Uliana paced back and forth while waiting in the personnel carrier. She could very definitely hear the sounds of fighting outside, but she resisted the urge to investigate, instead biding her time in a spot where she could be found.

Soon there came a soft rapping at the hatch which then increased in both volume and rapidity. Before the woman could throw open the door it swung open, seemingly of its own accord. She backed up against the far wall and looked through the opening, unsure of who or what she would find there.

In the haze of the snow and the biting cold of the Siberian air stood two of the valleymen, looking in at her. Their faces were sober, their eyes deadened.

Uliana said nothing. Wide-eyed, she stared back at the men, holding her self steady despite the frosty breeze that wafted in.

Then the two figures stepped up and into the vehicle and moved towards her with outstretched arms.

He soon lost track of how many of the strange warriors he'd downed. Stepping over the latest, who moaned softly on the ground below him, Captain Action moved on to the next battle.

The snow had begun to fall more heavily again and the temperature seemed to plummet. His muscles cried out with every swing of his sword, every kick he aimed at an invader, making him wish he could just sit down and catch his breath. The universe began to conspire against him.

He'd even had to fight a few of the Russian soldiers, who, and he forgave them for it, somehow lumped him in with the valleymen, though by sight alone the differences were staggering. Drake hated to have to raise a fist to these men, but the heat of battle had worked its way into their hearts and brains, and there was no stopping them with words.

He rounded a vehicle, and, through the snowfall, he could make out Marowit. The lieutenant was fighting viciously with one of the attackers, a larger specimen who carried two of the sickle-knives.

Marowit's own blades flicked in and out, countering jabs from his opponent and seeking openings through which to mount his own offenses. Both of the combatants were bloodied. Around them, Captain Action could make out the forms of soldiers yelling encouragements to the lieutenant, swinging their rifles around, perhaps looking for their own opportunities to end the fight, swiftly and surely.

Though the reputed "god of nightmares" was high on Drake's list of people who deserved a comeuppance, he winced at the wounds the man was taking in the fight.

Then suddenly a dark wall of valleymen plunged through the curtain of snow and fell atop the nearby soldiers. The entire scene broke up into twirling fits of chaos, a no-holds-barred melee that brought death to its fighters.

Captain Action hesitated, tried to make out exactly what was happening in the violent confusion, but all was obscured. The last thing he saw was Marowit go down, hard, and a valleyman pounce on the scarecrow of a soldier, knife sliding in and out of the pivot point of their struggle.

A lone figure sprinted across the battlefield and through the encampment. It wore a silver and blue uniform, not unlike a spacesuit or a high-altitude pilot's gear. On its head was a helmet with a large, clear faceplate.

The figure reached Captain Action's armored vehicle and swung around to its rear, finding the hatch there wide open and the cargo area empty. It climbed up and through the opening.

Making its way to a small door that separated the driver's area from the rest of the hold, the person went through that aperture and climbed into a seat. Gloved fingers toggled switches and clicked buttons, cycling through a variety of readouts. Within minutes, the figure seemed satisfied.

"That's one autopilot disconnected and out of a job," it murmured to itself.

Then a hum rose from the vehicle, a whirring of turbines or powerful engines. Outside large plates fell from the sides of the carrier, and then a massive portion of the roof popped up and fell to one side.

A valleyman who stood over a downed soldier looked up to see the armored vehicle seemingly explode. From within the resulting fireball came a smaller craft, shooting outwards and landing on three skids or skis that extended from its undercarriage.

The new vehicle skimmed over the snow and executed a perfect turn, then came to a halt. Save for its flat-bottomed ski legs, it was built along the exact same lines of Captain Action's Silver Streak and sported a completely enclosed, heated cockpit with a darkened windshield. The craft was painted in winter hues, almost perfectly blending in with the snow.

"Man," enthused the figure at its controls, "Will Robinson's got nuthin' on me..."

Colonel General Veles ran headlong at Captain Action, screaming and brandishing his Stechkin.

"Perun! At last you show yourself!"

The captain froze in place, with his lightning sword held aloft, glinting in the snowfall. He realized that the Russian commander had possibly gone mad from the battle.

Veles plowed into him with a grunt, knocking them both over into the snow, which was thrown up in the air by the impact.

"The lightning!" shrieked the huge man. "I will have it back! It is *mine* alone to command!"

He grabbed at the sword, a maniacal fervor etched into his face, his eyes. Drake brought the hilt of the weapon crashing down into the general's skull, effectively stunning him.

Captain Action got to his feet. Across from him, Veles mirrored the action, shaking off the blow to his head.

The general's eyes glistened as he took in the lightning sword. He'd been battling his way across the encampment when he spotted the American agent, and something within him snapped at the sight of Perun, the foe he'd been waiting for, holding *his* rune.

He *must* have the lightning back.

Drake sidestepped a charge from the general and clubbed him in the back of the head with the sword's pommel. This served to enrage the man, little else; and, like the bear that served as his country's symbol, Veles charged again.

The two men slammed together. The captain lashed out with his fists seeking for weaknesses, but the general's almost religious zealotry fueled him to the point of near invulnerability.

Captain Action went in with a savage chop of his hand to his opponent's larynx, but Veles caught the swing and both used leverage and Drake's own momentum to send him face-first into the ground.

"For *centuries* we have been at odds," the deranged general gasped out between wracking breaths. "But now, Perun, it will end! I will have what is mine, and you will trouble me through the ages no more!"

The captain looked up to see Flins and Juthrbog running towards them. He'd be outnumbered in seconds. Then Veles took a step, menacingly, then another, then rushed in for the kill.

He gripped the sword, ready to take whoever he could manage to Hell with him.

Uliana Ulanova walked across the frigid Siberian landscape between two valleymen. They guided her over to the survivors of the battle and left her there with them.

She looked all around her at the soldiers. Doing a quick headcount, she estimated that more than half the original Red Army force that had made its way to the barren place were gone, presumed killed in the struggle.

Incredibly, the Russians appeared none the worse for the wear. Some of them sported cuts or bruises, but they all stood on their own two feet and held the arms and legs in unbroken positions. It was as if they had been defeated in a way to keep them whole but for what purpose she could not guess.

Slowly, the valleymen returned and began forcing the soldiers into a line, two by two. Uliana was made to join them in that line, as if one of them.

Then the invaders moved them along, directed them to begin walking towards the north. The soldiers, cold and confused, offered little resistance. They pulled their winter uniforms tighter, put their heads down, and marched.

At the front of the line, Uliana made out four familiar figures. There strode Flins, Juthrbog, and a bloodied and bedraggled Marowit. Behind them walked Veles himself, his head down, limping slightly.

Trying to search up and down the line with her eyes while maintaining her stride, Uliana hoped to find yet one more familiar face, a far friendlier one.

But of Captain Action there was absolutely no sign.

X
UNDERGROUND

Like a funeral procession, the line of soldiers moved through the cathedral of trees, somber and silent. Those who were aware of the history of the area tried to imagine millions upon millions of trees on their sides, withered from the blast of the Tunguska explosion. Such thoughts cemented the funereal feeling of their march.

The Russian commanders at the front of the line grew less and less vocal in their protests, perhaps becoming more insensate from the cold and the alien beauty of their surroundings.

The valleymen themselves remained mute as they herded their prisoners along. Occasionally they prodded a straggler, but otherwise they walked along as if they, too, were hushed by the powerful, quiet majesty of the area.

The line continued on its way for the better part of the day and eventually came to a valley of sorts in the middle of the Siberian forest. The snow had stopped hours earlier and the landscape solidified in the view of the soldiers until the light began to disappear and nightfall brought an even greater chill.

Some of the men wondered how they would ever survive the night.

The valley dipped away from them, a broad bowl among the unending expanse of trees. The strange invaders did not halt to survey its expanse, but kept the line moving and descended along with their captives. The crisp air seeped into the soldiers' lungs and dulled their senses further; many of them thought that death was no longer a possibility; it was now a certainty.

On their way down into the valley, they passed a bear. Not more than the length of an average felled *taiga* tree from them, it paused from its hunt for insects and stared at the procession. A few of the men thought perhaps it was an illusion, a trick of the fading light and the increasing cold, since the beast all but ignored their intrusion on its dinner plans.

Then before they knew what was happening, the line marched first into a kind of rift in the landscape and then between a series of huge rocks.

71

They had entered blindly and unknowingly into a cavern.

The natural tunnel swallowed the soldiers whole. Wide enough to allow for four men to walk abreast, it dipped slightly downward into the earth. Ahead of the men was a dull light, illuminating the passage just enough for them to look around at the strange sights that flooded their awareness.

Further down into the earth the tunnel began to grow welcomingly warmer. Because of the phenomenon, the soldiers began to awake from what seemed like a year's slumber. An unusual scent came to their noses, too. It was earthy and almost sweet, a kind of smell that might remind some of farming or agriculture.

Then as if in answer to their unspoken questions, the passageway widened and the men saw plant life, inexplicable and strange, all around them.

Not roots, not the trailing ends of seeking shoots from foliage above sticking through the ceiling of dirt and rock over their heads, but cultivated plants. They grew in large recesses in the tunnel walls, pockets of dirt and soil that were like miniature gardens or farms. As the line passed the plants, some of the valleymen reached out and brushed their fingertips along the leaves and stalks, humming slightly as they did so.

The soldiers could easily tell then that the valleymen had come home.

Eventually the tunnel opened up into a chamber.

Marched almost to the center of the rocky cavern, the soldiers were motioned to stop. Then they craned their necks and rubbed their eyes and looked all around them.

The ceiling of the chamber was surely more than a hundred feet over their heads and the overall width of the room was at least double that. Large, crudely wrought, seemingly metal posts were set equally spaced around the circumference of the chamber and atop them hung baskets of a sort. From inside the baskets issued a glow that provided weak illumination.

Plant life filled the outer edges of the chamber. The combined scents from the display were almost overwhelming to the soldiers, so heady was the fragrance. There were edible examples, such as vegetables and fruits, but there was also bizarre growth that the men did not recognize and could not fathom its purpose.

Among the surprising plethora of flora there could be seen more valleymen of both genders. They wore less than the warriors who had fought on the surface above, eschewing the strange armor and heavy fur boots and gloves for more decorative pieces over their black coveralls. The entire ensemble seemed familiar, somehow, as if cobbled together from different surface sources. Their skin was pale, obviously a sign of underground life, and their hair ranged from dirty brown to grey-streaked black.

The valleymen plant-tenders looked up at the new arrivals with dull expressions then turned back to their work. The soldiers cast their eyes upon their fellows, unsure of what to think or believe about what was being presented to them.

"What is this place?" asked Colonel General Veles in a loud voice, speaking the thoughts of his men. His words rolled around in the chamber.

Some of his subordinates wheeled around, as if they had forgotten their commander was with them. So entranced were they by the subtle beauty of the experience of entering the underground chamber that they almost hated their general for speaking out loud and shattering the silence.

The odd inhabitants of the cavern didn't seem to care much for his voice, either. One of the warriors walked up to the man and glared at him.

Veles would have none of it. "I *demand* to know where we are and why! This is an outrage!"

The colonel general was abruptly cuffed on the side of the head for his apparent sin.

Flins jumped in to defend his commander and received a blow to the back of his head for the action. Marowit stood his ground, looking out at his captors through slitted eyes.

Veles turned back to his attacker, smiled wickedly at him.

"Your message has been received, Comrade." The general spoke then to his lieutenants. "We shall bide our time, which will soon come, and we will then eat our fill of revenge."

Flins glowered banefully, rubbing the back of his head. Juthrbog had walked over to one side of the chamber, apparently engrossed in the valleymen's cultivation of their crops. They did not stop him from looking, but watched him carefully.

A whine of turbines split the solitude of the frigid world outside and above the underground space. The unique craft that had been birthed from the shell of the general secretary's personnel carrier came zooming up on its skis, seemingly following the trail of the soldiers' march through the snow.

The craft stopped at the edge of the valley, and its pilot snapped open its canopy and climbed out. Turning in place, the helmeted figure looked all around and then reached back into the cockpit for a pair of binoculars.

Flipping open the helmet's faceplate, the figure peered through the lenses of the binoculars at the trail of the march. In the growing darkness, it was difficult to see anything, but at least the general direction of the line was still apparent.

The pilot clambered back into the craft, revved its engines, and began to descend into the valley. It hadn't gone but fifty feet before it was suddenly surrounded by the foreboding figures of the valleymen.

The craft came to a stop. The warriors advanced on it, closing in from all sides.

The pilot sighed behind the helmet. Thumbing the control stick, the figure sent the craft swiftly spinning in a wide arc, scattering the encroaching valleymen like tenpins.

Satisfied that the invaders were suitably subdued, the pilot looked all around the craft at their prone forms.

"Dummies..." came the whisper from beneath the helmet. Then the craft sped off on its way down into the valley.

The Russian captives were herded down another tunnel to a second underground chamber.

The new cavern was roughly the same size as the previous farming chamber but was vastly different in its layout. And it was even warmer.

Drafts of heated air blew over the faces of the soldiers, carrying with them an unusual smell of minerals and heated metals. It was not necessarily an unpleasant odor, but it was wholly strange to the men.

The chamber they stood in had no plant life but was illuminated in the same fashion as the previous area. Several openings in the cave walls ringed the cavern, tall enough for a man to walk through without stooping. Lights flickered from the openings and the sounds of metal against rock issued forth, too. Valleymen, wearing only an abbreviated version of their usual black material garment, filtered in and out of the doorways, carrying what appeared to be large digging tools of various kinds.

It was starkly obvious to the Russians that they were witnessing a mining operation.

Farther down the main chamber, the soldiers could see a massive platform, one that they realized with a start was as alien to the underground complex as they were to its inhabitants.

The platform rested roughly twenty or so feet above the cavern's floor on a spidery metal framework that clearly originated in the outside world. Atop it sat what could only be described as a series of metal huts with straight, slanted roofs and human-sized doors with handles. There were no windows they could see in the structures.

Along a railing that stretched across the entire platform stood seven unusual figures.

The men, if that was what they were, wore silvery-white suits that covered them from neck to foot and belted securely at their waists. Heavy protective gloves and boots covered their hands and feet; the look was reminiscent of emergency airfield fire crews or high-voltage workers. Their belts were studded with outlets and connection points, dials and controls. Tubes and wires ran from sections on the belts to either a bulky backpack they wore or to lighted panels that dotted the surfaces of the huts.

On their heads the figures wore large helmets, which were fashioned, apparently, to look like abstract human skulls. On the front of the gleaming white helmets a large, round port rested, covering the space normally taken up by eyes, nose and mouth, and looking like nothing less than one, dark singular eye.

The overall effect of the figures' garb was chilling. Their cyclopean eyes seemed to take in everything, unblinking and wholly inhuman.

Some of the figures stood operating the panels on the outside walls of the huts, while the others simply faced the chamber and looked out over it. If they took any notice of the arrival of the soldiers, no real sense of it could be discerned.

Then one of the white-suited men pointed out at the Russians, turned to a compatriot and seemed to converse. A moment later, two of the figures began to walk down a long metal staircase on the far end of the platform and to the chamber below.

Uliana Ulanova opened the collar of her coat and let the warmth of the underground air spread over her, suffusing her shapely form. Still standing at the back of the group of soldiers, she observed her surroundings and remained silent, the loss of Miles Drake surprisingly foremost in her thoughts. The men on the platform also troubled her greatly, but she held her tongue, unsure of what actions she would or should take, or even which might be available to her.

She watched as the two suited figures approached the soldiers, and then stopped some ten or fifteen feet from them. Without taking their single orbs off the group, they each extended one arm to their sides, pointing and making quick gestures to the nearby valleymen. In a moment, a folding set of a table and chairs were brought out and set up.

Uliana could not believe her own eyes. It was as if, perhaps, a picnic lunch was to be provided and cards and cigars brought out, so casually did the alien figures seat themselves and set their gloved hands on the tabletops.

But it quickly became apparent that that was not to be the case.

The valleymen shuffled the soldiers into a single line before the table, then shoved them one by one before the two suited men.

The great dark eyes on the helmets observed each Russian silently, then one of the figures pointed to either the left or to the right. Once a determination had been made, the soldier was led off to that side, forming two separate groups.

"They are putting us before a selection," said the man in front of Uliana. It dawned on her that it was the little myopic sergeant they called Skrzak.

"Like the Nazis in the camps, during the war," he whispered, turning around to look at the woman. His hands shook as he spoke. "None of us will survive this."

Before Uliana could reply, a shouting came from the front of the line, ringing through the cavern despite the sounds of mining in the distance.

It was Flins; the god of death refusing to take part in the proceedings.

One of the cyclopean figures stood up and motioned for the valleymen warriors. They came in on the lieutenant from both sides and proceeded to beat him savagely.

Veles said nothing, staring at the men at the table with cold fury in his eyes.

Finally, they paused in their blows and stepped back from the prone form of Flins.

The colonel general cleared his throat. "For every time you and these…. *things*," he said to the unblinking ports of the men, "have laid hands on my men, I will exact a payment."

Flins crawled to his feet, shakily, but then stood at attention by his commander's side. Blood flowed down from his temples, pooling in the collar of his uniform.

"We are *soldiers* in the army of the Union of Soviet Socialist Republics and will not stand for…"

Just then, a door on one of the huts opened and a man stepped through it and out onto the tall platform.

He wore a large white lab coat over a shimmering pair of blue silk pants and small black boots. Almond-shaped eyes and a yellowish cast to his skin denoted his Asian heritage. His hair was jet black and receding atop his round, fleshy face.

The man smiled slightly, blinking his eyes.

"Greetings," he addressed the group in flawless Russian. "I am Dr. Ling."

He gripped the platform's railing with meaty hands. "I apologize most sincerely for the manner in which you were brought to this place, but we did not, ahh, require *all* of you to join us here.

"You see, gentlemen, I am in need of miners."

Looking then squarely at Veles, he smiled again.

"General, please inform your men that they now work for *me*."

XI

ENGINEERING

"This, I will never do," responded the Russian commander, making a broad, sweeping gesture in front of his own bulk with one outstretched hand. He looked up at the man on the platform with clear defiance. "I think, though, that I will have answers instead!"

The Asian man continued to smile. "To common, garden-variety questions such as 'Why am I here?' or 'What is this place?' or, perhaps, the ever popular 'Who, sir, are *you*?'

"Alas, these are questions I do not overly care to answer. I have no desire to answer, especially, to a *Soviet*."

He swiveled around to motion to one of the helmeted figures, who then approached him. Dr. Ling looked at the singular eye of his subordinate, and the man behind it stared back. A strange, silent communication passed between them, and then Ling turned back to the prisoners.

"My engineers will see you to a place of rest," he said evenly, "but do not become too comfortable. You have much work ahead of you. Good day, Commander, to you and your men."

Interestingly, Veles offered no further retorts or outbursts, but nodded knowingly to his lieutenants and said no more.

As the Asian man began to turn to go back into his hut, his eye seemed to catch upon something in the cavern below him.

Or someone.

He stopped, then narrowed his eyes, fixated on one spot among the gathered Russians.

Uliana Ulanova had never felt so exposed in her life as when the odd figure focused his attention at that moment on her and her alone.

"There," said Ling, pointing. "That one there. That...*woman*. Bring her here."

A stirring among the soldiers then also caught the man's attention. He swiveled around to take in the huddled officers at the front of the mass of prisoners.

Ling frowned. "You have something to say, commander? You...*object*

"There. That one there. That...woman. Bring her here."

to my orders?"

A palpable hope seemed to emanate from the man, hope that the Russian general did truly object and so would be perhaps fair game for some sort of further deviltry.

Veles shook his head, glared daggers at a visibly agitated Juthrbog.

"Why should *I* object, Comrade? It is very clear that you have the authority here to do as you wish, *da*?"

He indicated his albino lieutenant. "It was only this fool here that you heard. Perhaps *he* has an objection?"

"Enough!" cried Ling, turning again to his helmeted accomplice. "Bring her up here and take them to their fate!"

And with that he wheeled around on his heel, stalked back into the metal structure and closed its door behind him.

While the soldiers were being herded en masse from the audience chamber and down one of the darkened subterranean passageways, a strange thing occurred.

As they departed, their general whispered to them surreptitiously to be ready for any sign from him, a sign that would signal rebellion. The message was passed down the line until every Russian possessed the knowledge that they would not go easily to their labors. They would wait for the sign.

Through the alien world they marched, kept in place by its odd inhabitants who shuffled along beside them and who also fell under the unblinking artificial eyes of the so-called "engineers." But this was not to last for long.

One of the valleymen came to pause in his gait and, with a bewildered expression on his pale face, looked at his hands, his arms, and across his body.

Then he looked up and all around himself. Pain crawled across his countenance, and he howled.

Everyone stopped, Russians and valleymen alike. The latter looked at their moaning fellow and then at each other. It was as if a great weight or a heavy shroud had been lifted from them. One soldier noticed tears in the eyes of the valleyman who stood next to him.

But of the greatest interest to the prisoners was the fact that their shepherds all threw their sickle-blades down onto the rocky floor of the passageway.

Veles' hands, both of them, shot up above his head. He shouted in a loud, commanding voice.

"Now, Comrades – *now!*"

Before the engineers could react to the new development, the soldiers broke formation and attacked their guards. In seconds the underground passageway was engulfed in booming, roiling chaos.

The valleymen were not so filled with apparent pain or remorse that they would not defend themselves. They howled all the more, to be certain, and drove fists and knees into the oncoming Russians. The soldiers, all trained in hand-to-hand combat, gave as good as they got, though.

The colonel general and his three lieutenants did not attack with the others. Veles said something to Flins and together the two of them approached one of the engineers, cautiously, but with obvious intent to subdue or worse.

The skull-helmeted figure turned to witness the Russian's approach. With almost graceful calm, the man twisted a control on his belt. Veles, seeing this, reared back. Flins dived for his target.

Gas of some malevolent variety poured from vents on the engineer's belt; from the belts of all the engineers present, in fact. Blue-green and sans odor, it snaked swiftly over and through the Russians, as if carried by a nonexistent wind.

In the blink of an eye, a paralyzing effect took hold. The men's senses remained active, sight, sound, smell, and the rest, but they were otherwise completely incapacitated by the strange vapor. And left standing in place like statues.

Astonishingly, the valleymen were not impacted by the gas. They stood and watched as their opponents succumbed to it, as if perhaps they knew the score and were waiting to take their own lumps.

Then a sonorous tone sounded throughout the caverns.

It seemed to have no single source, but rang around the soldiers quite clearly. Some of them even thought they could feel it on a different level than with just their ears, possibly as a vibration through the very rock on which they stood, frozen.

The eyes of the valleymen seemed to glaze over once again, and they turned in place to face the engineers.

"The soldiers are to be taken directly to the mines," said a loud voice, seemingly emanating from the engineers themselves.

"That is all. Carry on."

Doctor Ling smiled to himself as he closed the circuit on the panel in front of him and removed an unusual headset from his skull. Setting it down on a small hook, he got up from his chair and turned to his guest.

"I think they will be of no further trouble to me," he said. "My engineers can be quite persuasive."

Uliana looked around the room they now stood in. She'd been brought up to the platform and prodded up its staircase and into one of the metal huts, and there she found the Asian man in the lab coat, who shushed her the moment she entered through the door.

She stood and watched along with the doctor as the brief scrap between the soldiers and their captors played out on a large round monitor screen set into his console. Uliana was nigh mesmerized by the event and the manner in which it was settled, guessing that the monitor showed views from the engineers' helmets.

Now she took the time to actually study the inside of the hut.

If Action Mountain was a cave of wonders, this was a chamber of horrors, she thought.

Along one wall was a setup that in some ways resembled a medical bay, while in others appeared as a vivisectionist's playroom. Cabinets full of wicked-looking surgical equipment surrounded an adjustable table that featured large straps and a wooden block for a headrest. The entire surface of the table was covered what seemed to be dried blood.

Nearby sat a virtual jungle of a laboratory; vile-looking liquids burbled and bubbled in beakers and vials next to other queer substances that defied easy description, all of them foul-smelling and radiating with a strange warmth.

One corner of the room held a small bestiary. Cages and tanks contained all manner of wildlife and plant life, many of them obviously neglected. Uliana could make out lumps in some of the cages that she guessed to be animals. She wasn't sure and did not want to venture any closer to find out. Feeble sounds of mewling and coughing issued from the corner, too.

In the center of one wall a large opening in the metal siding exposed an entrance to a tunnel. The passageway beyond slanted downward into darkness, with a soft breeze blowing up through it.

The rest of the room was taken up with an array of consoles and panels, screens and readouts. The lighting was low throughout, so the electronics of the equipment provided an eerie feeling to the entire setting.

"I did not bring you here to admire my work area," hissed the doctor. "But now that you are here you should know that it is an honor bestowed upon you to view it."

Uliana's fingers curled and uncurled. "You expect me to be intimidated by all this?" she spat at the man.

"No, my dear. But believe me; if I were attempting to intimidate you, you would well know it," Ling said patiently. "Now, who are you?"

The woman stared back defiantly, then stepped forward and pointed directly at the man.

"You don't belong here!"

Ling grinned and nodded. "A strange statement, coming from one such as you, who came to this area with invaders?"

"I am Captain Kalla Lebedotchka, attached to the..."

"You are lying. Where is the man with whom you came to Siberia?"

The question surprised Uliana, then sobered her. Denials slithered to the tip of her tongue, but she muttered out the truth instead.

"Dead, so far as I know."

Ling looked long and hard at her with his almond eyes. "You are telling me the truth – or what you believe is the truth. So, then – now we will talk of *other things...*"

The blue and silver figure holstered his sidearm and glanced down at the man still twitching at his feet. Across from him lay three more men, all prone and unconscious.

Walking past the sleeping valleymen, the pilot of the snow craft searched for some signs of their passage through the area; he'd been exhaustively surveying the locale when he and his vehicle had been waylaid. Four quick bursts from his pistol later and he was able to continue his quest undisturbed.

At last he spied what looked like a footprint in the snow, then another and another. Following them, the pilot walked for a quarter mile, then suddenly found himself in a cleft in the rocky ground. There before him was a hole, dark and foreboding.

The figure unclipped a small tube from his belt and pointed it back at his vehicle. With a whirring click and a beep from the device, the craft's turbines ceased activity and its canopy closed on its own.

With a huge sigh, the pilot tramped into the cleft and into the cave entrance, on his way downward. Marveling at how well hidden it was from the surface and, most likely, from the air, he also wondered how, in the armpit of Siberia, it had ever been found in the first place.

Finally, the Russian prisoners were marched into a larger cavern, one which quite literally took their breath away.

As they looked around at the momentous sight before them, the men almost forgot their predicament, so alien and awe-inspiring was it.

Some hundred or more meters tall, the chamber's ceiling at first appeared to be an immense, sprawling stained glass window designed by a mad artist. Rivulets of glowing illumination in the rock stretched from one end of the cavern to the other, and there gathered into a massive carbuncle of muted light. The multicolored veins ran haphazardly to their conjoined ending place, and the entire mass then seemed to disappear into the rock of the chamber, high above its floor.

The light from the spectacle was of a sickly variety, almost pulsing in some areas and seemingly flowing in others. It gave off an unhealthy impression, despite the wonder of its arrangement across the cavern's ceiling.

Below where the glowing mass disappeared into the wall, the soldiers could see a concentration of mining shafts. In and out of the shafts drifted valleymen, carrying baskets of rocks of varying size and shape.

With dire recognition, and with little or no experience of it, the men knew they were in the presence of irradiated strata. And that the mysterious Dr. Ling intended for them to mine it.

The Asian man's engineers directed the valleymen guards to bring tools for the soldiers to begin their task.

"There is something...*different* about you, apart from your sex," said Ling. "You are *with* the soldiers, but you are not *of* them. This is very apparent to me."

"Please," implored Uliana, eyeing the man and wary of her tone. "Tell me what is going on here."

She considered her strategy for a moment, weighing factors.

"I feel as if there is danger from radiation in this area. Aren't you concerned about being contaminated by staying here?"

The doctor looked at her even more carefully, stepping closer as he did so. Uliana was reminded of a lizard, for reasons she couldn't fathom. There was even a kind of smell about him that reinforced the perception.

"You are, perhaps, an expert on radiation, hmm?"

She suddenly felt weak, very weak and weary.

"Yes, yes; I can see that now," he continued, closing his eyes. "Splendid. Let me tell you of my findings, then, and of my conundrum.

"These caverns are infused with the emissions of a specific breed of particles, a variety I have never encountered before. The wave signature, I have discovered, is unique, also."

Uliana's head swam. She felt as if she were underwater; her breathing had become labored and her sight clouded.

"It is, I feel, not akin to true radiation, but, my dear, are you well?"

When Ling turned to look at her, she saw only his eyes. All else was dark, save for his penetrating eyes, looking into her, *through* her, as if she had no clothes, no skin covering her.

She felt suddenly very alone.

Something bumped into her back. It slowly dawned on her that she'd been backing away from the doctor and walked into his bloodstained table.

"I am mining for what I refer to as the 'heart' of the matter, the focal point for the radiation in this region. Humorously, I keep coming across other precious metals, but not the precious material I covet.

"I sense," he continued, "that *you* hold information that is pertinent to my operations here. I sense that you know more about this place than even I do.

"Now, why would that be?"

Trying to move around the table, but not daring to turn away from the man, she held out one hand to hold him back. Her fingers brushed against his lab coat and an abrupt, instantaneous wave of revulsion lanced through her.

"Stay back," she ordered him, but the words were slurred. Looking out through tunnel vision, she saw Ling reach for something nearby.

Hands grasped her wrists, pushed them against something hard. Then, the same sensations at her ankles.

She suddenly felt like she was lying down. When had that happened?

The doctor filled her sight, with glowing eyes and a forked tongue. His head came within inches of hers, a heady smell of metal and chemicals flooding her nose.

Something was glinting off to one side. What was it?

A knife. No, a scalpel.

Hands touched her. She began to lose all feeling.

"Well, well," said Dr. Ling, his words laced with wonder. "What do we have here?"

XII
INFORMATION

She hadn't been brought back. It had been too long. Something was very wrong.

He got to his feet, shrugging off the stiff piece of material that passed for a blanket in the underground world. All around him lay utterly exhausted Russian soldiers, asleep or as near to sleep as they'd achieve in such a strange, foreign place.

He moved. Unsure as to what he'd do or where he'd go, he moved because it was better than not moving. Not moving meant things weren't happening, and things needed to start happening.

Outside the small "room" they'd been shuffled into after many long hours working in the mines, he assumed there'd be guards. Whether it was the valleymen or the engineers, he wasn't sure, but he was about to find out.

A strong hand reached out from the almost perfect darkness and grasped his arm. He swiveled in place, ready to strike, ready to free himself.

A ghostly face came forward. Juthrbog.

"It's as I suspected," said the albino Russian lieutenant, matter-of-factly. "You're going out to find her?"

The man watched as his commander shrugged off his coat and then removed his face.

An incredible change took place. Where once was Veles, god of the lightning and thunder, now stood a strikingly different figure.

"Captain Action," said Juthrbog, nodding in understanding.

"I need your help, Lieutenant," said Miles Drake, rolling up the plastiderm mask of the colonel general and secreting it in his belt. "*She* needs your help."

"You need me to distract our guards," came the calm reply as both men turned in unison and began heading for the entrance to their rest area. "One question: where is the colonel general?"

Captain Action looked at him somberly. "Dead."

"Perhaps that's for the best," commented the lieutenant.

He'd never meant to kill the man. For days he'd worked on the plastiderm mask, fashioning it in secret, even keeping Uliana in the dark about it. Drake thought of it as a bit of "insurance" in case the entire deal went sour and he needed to take over the expedition in a role of authority; if his part as the general secretary was exposed.

He hadn't intended for Veles to die. He didn't want the man to be impaled on his lightning sword. But in the heat of battle, things happen. The Russian had fought against him violently in a fit of insane rage, and...

Drake pushed the thoughts from his mind, focused on the problem at hand. Juthrbog, now seemingly an ally rather than an enemy, was speaking.

"I've scouted our situation. Two of the inhabitants of this place are stationed just outside the entrance. And from what I can glean, one of the suited men waits further down the passageway.

"I will handle one of our guards, if you take the other."

The captain stopped him, spun the man around to face him. "No deaths. No more deaths if they can be avoided."

The albino looked him in the eye, then blinked. "Understood. On the count of three?"

He was wrong to have allowed the beautiful woman to leave the group. He honestly thought that their captor would, oddly enough, treat her respectfully, that being with him was better somehow then possibly being forced to work in the mines.

Exhaustion was addling his brain, complicating things. He needed to focus, needed to be Captain Action. It might be the only way to get everyone through the dangerous hours, possibly the days that stretched out before them.

It had been a challenge for Drake to essay the role of Veles, balancing the man's uniquely brusque form of authority with his own agenda, but it was imperative for him to survey the problem at hand not as himself, but as someone who would attract no undue attention. The captain desperately needed the advantage of surprise where his present opponent was concerned and he hoped he still held that advantage. Everything depended upon it now.

And Juthrbog? There was the question of his allegiance, his supposed feelings for Uliana, but those would have to wait. For now.

He and the lieutenant approached the doorway to the rest chamber. A black curtain of the ever present material hung over it, covering it completely. Juthrbog slipped around it and called to one of the guards, as Captain Action watched covertly.

The valleyman sauntered over to the Russian. Then his fellow guard began to follow suit. Drake whipped the curtain from its holders and flung it over the head of the second man, then delivered a stunning chop to his neck. The form beneath the enshrouding curtain slumped and collapsed and he allowed it to slither to the ground.

Juthrbog was setting his own unconscious guard down on the floor of the cavern, too. Then the albino made a jerking motion with his chin, indicating that the A.C.T.I.O.N. agent should be on his way.

"Find her," said the Russian as Drake slipped past him. "Please."

Fifty or so feet down the shadowy natural passageway, he glimpsed one of the engineers standing at a junction of corridors. The suited, helmeted figure had his back to the captain.

He'd encountered the malevolent accomplices of his foe once before, in China, and had gained some small insight into their nature. Overall, though, they and their ties to their leader remained a mystery, but Drake knew one thing for certain: they were never completely out of contact with the man at any time.

The helmet was the key; its gigantic, staring eye port saw and told all.

Captain Action moved quickly and stealthily, the rubber soles of his boots specially designed for near silent movement. He had one chance to subdue the engineer; if that was botched, he'd bring the whole house of cards down upon his head and everyone else's.

He dove at the suited figure, slipped one arm around its neck, applied pressure. The man's hands shot up to grab his arm and applied pressure of their own.

The two struggled in silence. Captain Action gritted his teeth to keep from yelling out from the pain being applied to his arm. With his other hand he smeared soil from the damp floor of the passageway over the giant eye, then slipped that same hand up and underneath the helmet, searching for a seal or the edge of a collar.

It was a test of wills. The engineer tried to slam his attacker against the cavern walls, but Drake leveraged his body away with one leg. It was a precarious position; at any second they could both tumble to the ground and lose their holds on each other.

Then, abruptly, he found skin and muscle and nerve endings up under the helmet and dug in with his strong fingers.

Finally, the engineer went rigid, then collapsed.

He wasted precious little time in trying to get the man's helmet off. Searching for and not finding a strap or a release of some kind, he simply pulled at it. The helmet stayed annoyingly in place.

Drake looked all around him, senses heightened, clear on the fact that he could be discovered at any second.

Then, slowly, inexorably, the large piece of headwear began to loosen. With a loud *splortch*, it came off its owner's head and he gazed down at the face underneath.

The man was human, or at least the captain guessed he was. Pale, blue-tinged skin stretched tautly over his skull, darkly spider-veined and malignant-looking. The man's ears were almost non existent and his eyes, which were still open, were white and blank as coddled eggs.

There were also round, indented marks around the circumference of his head, grotesquely slick with some smoky, viscous liquid. Seeing them, Drake quickly upended the helmet and looked inside.

There he saw some sort of connection points which seemed to correspond to the marks on the engineer's skull. *Always in contact, till death do them part*, he thought to himself.

Captain Action proceeded to remove the man's suit, boots, gloves, and belt, then dragged the prone figure and stuffed him in a craggy recess in the wall of the corridor. After putting on the garments, he paused and stared down into the helmet once more. He reached in and, one by one broke off each connector point.

Then, cautiously, he placed the helmet on his own head.

It's only another role, he told himself. *Just another role!*

The captain, disguised as an engineer, moved down the passageway and into the maze of tunnels. The eye port in front of his face was thankfully clear, allowing him to see where he was going. He surmised that shutting down its electronics made it just another piece of glass.

He also chided himself constantly on every single action, every movement he made.

Don't hurry; don't worry, he said in his head. You're an engineer; you belong here.

And "here" was one incredible place.

Above and beyond the danger he was in, the peril that every single soldier of the expedition and Uliana herself were in, he marveled at the subterranean world into which he'd been dropped.

It was far more than he expected, even imagined in his execution of the mission. But it was all tied up in the place; the valleymen, the radiation, the unwelcome presence of his foe, everything. He just had to untie the knot and get it all sorted out.

Recalling his mental notes on the directions he'd made when he and the soldiers were brought to the mines, he backtracked as well as he could and prayed he hadn't made a wrong turn. Passing a few of the valleymen, he realized that he must be holding himself up properly as an engineer because they all avoided him like the plague.

Then, turning a corner, Drake entered into the audience chamber and saw its towering platform before him.

Moving up onto and then across the platform like he owned it, Captain Action determined which of the huts was the one that he'd seen the Asian man come out of earlier, then, steeling himself, opened the door and slipped inside.

Darkness enveloped him. Ahead of him sat a large bank of blinking lights and telltales surrounding viewscreens and monitors. The yellowish chair in front of the array was empty. He seemed to have found no one home.

He began to turn to search the rest of the area when he heard a soft moan drift over to him. The low exhalation of breath whispered through the room, made even more audible by the helmet's audio capabilities.

It had come from somewhere to his left.

Miles Drake's heart sank. With a sense of dread washing over him, filling him with one of the sickest feelings he'd ever experienced, he turned and looked.

There, against one wall, in a halo of weak light from a spot that hung down from the ceiling, a woman was strapped to a table. She moved her head from side to side, issuing the moan he'd heard.

Uliana.

But an Uliana that was otherworldly to him. Instead of her short, black mop of hair, long gorgeous golden tresses fell down around her neck and shoulders.

"Golden" was an understatement, he thought. Her hair was brilliant, almost blinding, even in the weak light. It shone like the sun, if the sun could be contained in human hair.

Numb, Drake stumbled over to her. Stripped to the waist, Uliana sported numerous deep and shallow cuts across her arms, sides, and stomach. There were also intravenous lines tapped into her at several spots; her breathing was shallow, too, and her complexion much lighter than her normal tawny coloration.

He fumbled at the straps which bound her to the table, tears coming to his eyes. He blamed himself immediately. Who else was responsible for the mistreatment, save for the man who had violated her in this room?

"Oh, Yu-Yu…" he said quietly, having freed one wrist and working on the other.

Ashamedly, he could not stop staring at her golden locks. He was at a loss to guess at what it meant.

Then the door to the hut opened and its proprietor entered.

"What is the meaning of this?" spat Dr. Ling, apoplectic at the sight before him. "What are you doing? *Explain yourself!*"

Captain Action realized he still wore the full garb of one of the man's engineers. Releasing the woman's wrist, he stood up straight and turned to face the doctor, wondering if there was any way out of this newest wrinkle.

"Come here!" ordered Ling.

Drake obeyed. Walking slowly, in the smooth manner of an engineer, he approached his most heinous foe, but stopped short of coming too close. He could see the reaction in the doctor's eyes and smiled to himself. Timing, timing…timing was always an issue.

Ling's mouth opened, ready to hurl an oath.

The A.C.T.I.O.N. agent tore off his helmet and hurled it at the man instead.

The heavy, domed headgear smashed headlong into Ling's face, squarely between his eyes. He reeled backwards violently, falling over the chair that rested in front of the bank of monitors.

Captain Action dived through the air, got his hands around the man's neck, and squeezed.

"Hello, *Doctor*," he hissed through his teeth. "Funny place to find you in."

The Asian man's slanted eyes widened, nearly popped out of his skull. "*You!*"

For every action, there is an equal and opposite reaction. This is taught in schools across the globe, as well as in alleyways and in the dirty streets of the cities of the world. It is a truism.

Dr. Ling's reaction to his opponent's chokehold was to not spare a second in witty repartee, but to drive his meaty fingers and lacquered fingernails directly into the man's eyes.

Both stunned and in pain, the two combatants released each other and went to their respective corners.

Drake blinked furiously, stabbing fury cutting across his eyes. Dr. Ling rubbed at his throat, stumbled away from his enemy, favoring a leg that had been twisted from his fall.

"Physical altercations," he said, "are distasteful to me. But for *you*, I will always make an exception."

He came in straight, chopping at Captain Action with an extended hand seemingly made of iron. The blow caught the nearly-blind agent on the temple. He grunted, staggered by the force of it.

Drake tried to think through what devices might be on the engineer's belt, or built into it, but he had to admit that he hadn't really ever been able to study up on them.

So fisticuffs it was. He went in low and swinging.

The two men, for lack of a better term, whaled on each other. When they finally broke apart, both of them recognized at the very same time that, all present factors considered, neither one of them was gaining any ground.

"My engineers, my Seven," hissed Ling, "are on their way, Captain."

The doctor apparently felt no further words were necessary. He had the upper hand and he knew it.

"This is *my* kingdom. My *empire*!

"*You* are the outsider here. You are the unimaginative barbarian at the gates."

Captain Action wiped a trickling stream of blood from his nose, risked a look back at Uliana.

"Why, damn you?! What do you think you have to gain here? You don't do anything without it gaining you something!"

The doctor smiled. His face, incredibly, was unbruised, unbloodied. Though he panted and wheezed and was bent over from exertion, he showed no overt, visible signs of damage from the battle.

"Why," he said, "there's *much* here to gain, my friend. You need but look around you. This, as I said, is the empire I've needed all along, a place from which I may strike at the world and never worry about exposing myself.

"And you well know that one such as I was not made to exist out in the open, hmm?"

Drake walked backwards, towards the woman still strapped to the table. He began to pull cords and lines from her, one eye still on Ling.

"Those people out there, what are you doing to them? They don't deserve your brand of oppression. You're killing them."

His foe paused in his advance towards the table. Coming up out of the darkness and into the halo of light, he reminded the captain of Satan coming up out of the Pit.

"Oh, I've tried to give you the benefit of the doubt before, my captain, but your lack of intelligence still shocks me.

"These people? The ones who mill about here and do my bidding? *They are dying*, my friend. They are, for the most part, the walking dead."

Captain Action squinted, peered intently at the man. "The radiation? But, I thought…"

"You 'thought.' A dangerous proposition for a member of a species so low on the evolutionary scale. Here, let me give you one more vital piece of information."

Ling reached out for a control. Drake started, began to shout at him.

"No, this you really must see, Captain."

He shut off the spotlight over the table.

In the sudden darkness, Uliana glowed like a firefly.

XIII
CITY

The sixty-fifth Bury hurried along through the warren of tunnels, juggling thoughts of his kinsmen with apprehension for the Eyes. But he had been called and when he was called he went, heedless of his own safety.

And these were times when safety was nothing to throw away.

In dress and in physical makeup, the man appeared much the same as his kin, with dirty brown hair and sunken eyes and pale skin, but there was an aura about him that, should one look more closely, betrayed his status as one of the Free. Bury wasn't certain what skein of fate was woven to gift him with such a position, but he never took it for granted and, in turn, never refused a plea for aid.

He knew things, did Bury. The stores of knowledge in his head were said to be vast, far more than that of an average dweller, and, before the Eyes came, he was often approached for his opinion, his insight and his ability to tell a good tale. Now things were different and the calls for help were few and far between.

But that made them all the more important, he often told himself. Like that one that came just a quarter cycle ago, one that he couldn't ignore; it had taken him that quarter cycle just to check on his surroundings and make certain he could make the run without endangering others.

Out of the City he flew, avoiding the rotations of the Taken and, hopefully, ducking from the Eyes. Bury headed toward the Up, near the Gardens, where more of the Free awaited him and someone else.

"Thank you for coming," said the Seventy-First Sing. Bury clasped hands with the elder man and they lightly slapped each other around the face in greeting. Sing was also one of the Old Names, a position growing increasingly rare, thought Bury.

He nodded and held his palms up and opened to his kinsman. "For me, there is no other way. Of course I came. No need to thank me for it."

"It's getting harder to call you," said Sing, "and even harder to stay Free. Here, in the Gardens, we..."

Bury cut him off, not caring much for how rude he might appear. "With respect, that can wait. Where is he? I'll have to be back before the Address and time slips by so quickly."

The older man blinked his eyes in agreement, then turned and ushered Bury down a narrow cleft in the passageway wall. Soon they were enveloped in darkness.

Up ahead Bury could see flickering light. Behind Sing he entered into a small, low-ceilinged chamber, one he recognized as a place he'd played in as a boy. Some things never change, he thought to himself.

"Mix, Tunnel, see who I've brought. He's here to meet the young man."

Sing stepped out of the way to reveal two kinsmen, younger bucks who Bury wasn't as familiar with. The two frowned at him, simply nodding in greeting and saying nothing.

Then they themselves stepped to the side and Bury saw their acquisition.

He was, as Sing had said in his message, a young man, at least twelve turn-cycles or more. He wore a wondrous garment of brilliant blue and silver, far brighter than any hues that Bury had ever seen in his lifetime, even Above. The young man had a look of great concern on his face, but he stepped up to Bury with assurity, perhaps even with a touch of bravado.

"Hello," he said, extending a hand, "I'm Sean Barrett and I'm looking for Captain Action. Have you seen him?"

Soon after, as Bury drifted through the underground chambers, he tried to coalesce his thoughts into something that resembled a straight line. The young man in the room he'd just left complicated things and things were about as complicated as they'd been in a thousand years or more.

At first the dwellers couldn't understand the small stranger. He spoke in a strange language and much too quickly, and as he did he grew more agitated at his inability to make himself understood. But Bury and Sing soon calmed him down and, through trial and error and some expressive pantomime, got to the root of the young man's plea.

He was trying to find one of the other recently arrived strangers from Above.

Bury knew where that stranger was, he thought, through the connections he maintained with the Free. And as soon as he realized what the young man wanted, Bury sped off on his newest mission.

He'd seen the gaggle of strangers when they were first brought in, as he walked through the Gardens just a cycle ago, playacting as one of the Taken. He almost gave himself away, staring at the procession, but he regained composure and stored away the memory for future pondering.

Well, now he had something he could use those thoughts for. Maybe.

The white-suited stranger grabbed his shoulders and stared at him with great intent.

"Say that again," he urged.

"I said," began Bury again, "that I bring you a message."

He'd slipped into the temporary rest area with little to no trouble, for he used an access point not known but to a few. It was one of those tunnels that one didn't see if one came at it a certain way but would suddenly appear if approached from a different direction and a different mind-set.

Looking around at the slumbering figures in the prison chamber, he saw one who was not sleeping. His clothes, pale and ghostly, looked nothing like those of the others, and he seemed to match the rough description they'd eked out of the boy. The man showed intriguingly little surprise when approached, almost eager for action of any mettle.

Interestingly, Bury could just understand the stranger, unlike the boy. To be completely honest, he could understand a fair portion of what he was saying, and, conversely, that seemed to hold true for the man himself. There were seemingly common roots to their languages, enough to, with patience, make themselves somewhat clear to each other.

And the stranger seemed to be quite good at learning and remembering.

"From a friend, I assume. He wants to see you, as soon as possible."

But with that, things broke down a bit. The handsome stranger, Bury found he envied the good color in his hair and skin, was having trouble at the moment and looked back him with growing confusion and frustration.

"He wants to see me, huh?" said the man, disgustedly. "But on his terms this time, no doubt. If only I knew how Uliana is. If I could…"

Now Bury felt himself growing confused. Hadn't he brought good news? Weren't these strangers as gregarious as his kinsmen? Didn't he want to hear from his friend?

"I'll just take you there," he told the stranger, and reached out to take his arm and make a gesture indicating, he hoped, exiting. He had directed Sing to move the young man secretly to the City, and there have him wait for Bury to return. If he could just get this stranger there before the Address.

The man's eyes narrowed. Bury could see him set his jaw and grow apprehensive, but he was determined to bring about the meeting and, in some small way amid the chaos, bring a little light into the Below. Then, perhaps, Bury could be of use; he'd already lost so much over the turn-cycles of his life and yearned to make amends with the universe.

Maybe then it would stop caving in on him.

He had to admit it to himself: the sight of the sickly glow suffusing Uliana had knocked him for a loop.

He'd been so rattled by it, down to his very core, that he'd lowered his defenses at that surreal moment and allowed his foe to poke him with some kind of drug. Next thing he knew, he was waking up back among the Russians and fielding some very, very tough questions from them.

But what of Uliana? There'd been women before in Miles Drake's life, of course, but their comings and goings had usually been pretty cut and dry. His feelings for Uliana, if that's what he could call them, were something more complicated. She got under his skin, past his disguises. If he was right, she saw through the roles.

Now this, whatever this was, he thought as he prepared to follow the odd valleyman through the shadows of the subterranean catacombs. As Captain Action, he had to first concentrate solely on rescuing the woman, then sorting the rest out later. It was a sobering thought: he had to survive his next meeting with his enemy, or there'd be no later.

"Hold on a moment," the captain said to his would-be guide. "Too conspicuous as is."

He flipped open his belt buckle and depressed a small button beneath it. A second later, a wash of color spread out from his belt and over his snowy uniform, transforming the entire ensemble from its pale whites and grays to the dark blues and blacks of his traditional gear. Now he lacked only his cap to make him feel he was once again operating as Captain Action, but the stand-in had been lost among the *taiga* when he'd hastily taken on the role of Veles.

Communicating with his guide was getting easier, though, thanks to his ability to quickly pick up languages and adapt to changing situations. With basic Russian as a foundation, plus what he'd picked up in dialect since they'd entered the country *and* some theories he had about the valleymen's makeup, he'd found a way to get his point across. Most times.

"What's your name?" he asked the man as they slipped past a phalanx of guards, left the area, and began moving. "My name is Miles."

"Bury," answered his guide.

"Then…you're an undertaker, perhaps?"

"No," said the man, looking quizzically over his shoulder at him. "I'm a teacher, of a kind." He said nothing further for a moment, lost in thought.

Then, "Ah, I see. How strange. No, my name doesn't reflect my life-task. I have a good friend named Heal who is only a builder in the City, you see, our names, many of them, no longer stand as Truth.

"For a recent example, once Up was only used for the Gardens, and the chamber in which they dig was Forbidden to the dwellers. But now, things are different and Truth no longer holds the soil as it once did like our names, especially the Old Names like mine."

It was utterly fascinating and Drake had a hundred more questions, but he chided himself for wasting time on it; nothing mattered more than finding Uliana and getting her to safety. If that meant confronting his foe face-to-face again, so be it.

He'd get to the bottom of the entire series of mysteries one way or another, preferably by the most direct route.

The city was far more than Captain Action had ever bargained for. As a concept, it was staggering.

That the underground complex of caverns and its inhabitants existed at all strained his sense of what the Earth could offer in terms of the fantastic, but an entire subterranean city threatened to dwarf him with wonder.

"This is New Lake," explained his guide. "This is our home."

Drake looked out over an immense, sprawling natural cavern, potentially one of the largest on, or in, the planet. In fact, as his brain began to decipher and interpret what he was viewing, he realized that what he was seeing was *multiple* caverns, all enormous.

Bury had led him through a passageway that dipped downward from the chambers they'd left, eventually exiting out into the city caverns. They stood together on a naturally formed landing, a dimple in the awe-inspiring formation of rock that surrounded the buildings, some few of them at least ten stories tall.

Yes, he thought to himself; I'm looking at *buildings*: actual buildings far below the Earth. It was incredible.

The structures appeared to be built up from the floor of the caverns using found stone, irregularly shaped rocks that were used like bricks to form walls and supports and ceilings and arches and streets. The overall look was of a gigantic opaque medieval mosaic of a city; a haphazard architectural choice that, surprisingly, worked. The buildings also looked strong enough to withstand the march of eons.

Many of the structures stretched upwards as far as to the ceilings of the great chambers, mingling with the humongous stalactites there and in some cases fully joined with them. Drake guessed that such an arrangement lent untold support to the buildings, a communion of the planet and that which mankind built upon it, or, in this case, *in* it.

The entire cityscape was lit from the glow of illumination from the sparse windows among the buildings, most likely the same as the first caverns he saw. There were also people, the valleymen, milling about the city here and there, going about their business with nary a sound.

He found himself leaning forward to try and take in more of the panorama that stretched out and away from where they stood. There, in the far distance, he spied where one chamber ended and another began, and the buildings that continued past those points. Where it ended he couldn't tell. New Lake was one of the most beautiful sights he'd ever beheld.

The style of some of the structures reminded Drake of the famous Cathedral of St. Basil in Red Square in Moscow, while others spoke of Eastern influences and even…yes, he was sure of it. Even Scandinavian designs from antiquity.

Over the entire city there hung a mist. It was a fine spray of moisture that floated around the tops of the buildings, not thick and heavy, but transparent and wraith-like.

Ideas floated through Captain Action's thoughts. He felt he was on the verge of understanding much, but witnessing the city, he also realized he knew so little.

A hand tugged at his sleeve, then more forcibly pulled at him. Looking over at a concerned Bury and then down to his own boots, Drake saw with a start that he was standing as close to the edge of the precipice as he could without falling.

"You'll fall," said his guide with urgency. "Step back and then we'll…"

A tone sounded. It was the same tone Drake had heard back in the other chambers. Something was about to happen.

"The Address!" hissed Bury. "Back! Back! Where we won't be seen! Hurry!"

Fitting themselves into the deep recesses of the landing, Captain Action and Bury were afforded a view of a balcony-type arrangement some fifty to seventy-five feet up above and over from their vantage point. Whoever would occupy the balcony would be hard-pressed, though, to see anyone on the landing.

At that moment, three figures walked out to its railing and stopped, looking down and over the city.

Glimpsing the central figure, the captain grew grim. It was Dr. Ling. And he had two of his engineers with him.

"I thought you were taking me to see him," he whispered stridently to Bury. "What's going on?"

The valleyman flapped one hand at Drake, not daring to take his eyes from Ling. "What? No! Now be quiet!"

The doctor's voice boomed out into the city chamber; at first he guessed that there was an amplification system he couldn't see, but it dawned on him that the engineers were most likely routing it through their amazing suits. Then, when he heard both Russian and the valleymen language come through simultaneously, the captain knew that the suited figures were also providing an almost instantaneous translation.

"Citizens, come forth," said Ling, gripping the balcony and standing tall and erect. Below, dozens of the underground inhabitants were filtering into a square or a large courtyard on the edge of the city that faced the balcony. Within a minute, it had become hundreds. They looked up at Ling with somber expressions.

'The work progresses, and I have brought in help from the outside world, but your participation must continue unabated. More workers will be needed to achieve our goals, for we are moving far too slowly.

"Many exciting discoveries have been made already. If we all work together we shall reap the benefits together, and I will be able to, as I have told you, help you to fulfill your promise as a society. But that will only come about with unselfish sacrifice and hard work. This is what I ask of you.

"I regret to say that I must also impose new restrictions on travel between the city and the outer chambers. Only those citizens cleared by me personally will be able to access certain sensitive areas. It is with a heavy heart that I make this announcement. There will be a posting of the details within one cycle, so that they will be clear to you all."

Captain Action watched the faces among the crowd as the doctor's words took hold. Some nodded blankly in agreement, while others stood as statues, their eyes dull and lifeless. There were also those few who within them a cold fury was being stoked.

"And on the important subject of postings, there will also be a list of further restrictions on certain words and phrases used in messages and correspondence, advertisements, and contracts.

"This is for your own good. Remember we must have harmony and a collective force of will to triumph over adversity. I do not place these restrictions on you lightly but do so because I and I alone can see the future that awaits us together. And in peace.

"Now, step forward, citizens."

Drake saw Ling turn to one of the engineers, who handed him a box. The suited figure then lifted up the box, leaving behind a queer apparatus in the doctor's hands.

It was a huge eye. The orb, as large as a melon, rose up on a twisted stalk of fleshy-looking cords and wires, unblinking and bloodshot.

Captain Action flinched, made to move forward. Bury caught his arm and dragged him back out of view.

The loud tone sounded again. Ling closed his own eyes and took a deep breath into himself. The iris of the grotesque object began to glow and then its pupil likewise.

Abruptly a third engineer appeared on the balcony. The doctor wheeled around, anger sparking across his face, but then he leaned into the man and they seemed to converse.

"Citizens," said Ling, turning back once more to his subjects. "Regrettably, my presence is urgently required elsewhere. I shall return in one-half a quarter-cycle."

And with that, he and his engineers were gone.

Before he could begin to process what he'd just seen and heard, Drake was being directed down a narrow, steep staircase cut into the rock wall of the city chamber. Bury informed him that there was little time to waste.

"Why do you allow this?" Drake asked the man. "I know this man. He means nothing, *nothing* but harm to you and your people."

"At first," said Bury soberly, not turning and still moving, "we were *taken* by him when he arrived one cycle. The look about him, his strangely pleasing face, his words. Many were pleased to find someone from Above so well-spoken and strangely familiar."

Captain Action wondered why Asian features might spark such interest in a people like the valleymen. Another avenue for exploration someday, when the crisis was over.

"Then, slowly, he began to take control of different facets of our lives."

"Yes, that's how it always begins. That's his way. Do you have a leader here, someone he deposed?"

"Well, I suppose, if I take your meaning, that Bring would meet that

The orb, as large as a melon, rose up on a twisted stalk of fleshy-looking cords and wires, unblinking and bloodshot.

definition, but, no, Bring is still one of the Free and still in the City."

Drake thought a moment. "Tell me, Bury; do the dwellers have a name they call the man that spoke on that ledge just now?"

"Yes," the man replied, pausing in his descent, but with his back still to the captain.

"We call him Evil."

In a basement room of one of the nearest buildings, a small gathering of the Free met. When they had exchanged both normal pleasantries and then concerns about the new edicts, they brought out a certain someone for Captain Action to see.

"Sean!"

He crushed the boy to him, bottled up emotion welling up and threatening to spill over. Sean Barrett rode the tide, glad to be back in his mentor's presence and, for a moment, put all his fears behind him.

Drake then looked at Sean and shook his head ruefully. "Now how many episodes of *Batman* have you missed?"

"Don't remind me," said the boy glumly. "Cap, what's going on here? That was *him* out there!"

"Not now, Sean. This isn't the right time. It will come; trust me. You have to trust me."

The boy was undeterred. "But he wants to *kill* you! I can't believe he hasn't done it already!"

"He just had the chance," said Drake, glumly. "For all his intelligence, he's a cold-blooded killer, but when he has me in his presence and he has something to torture me with, he'll keep me around. To toy with me sadistically."

Sean squinted, studying his mentor. "And does he, Cap? Have something over you?"

"Oh, yes," whispered the captain, shaking his head. "Yes he does."

The young man looked around, as if suddenly remembering something. "Wait…where's Yu-Yu?"

The beautiful defector and Sean had become close during the prepping of the mission, Drake remembered. Perhaps it wasn't just the overwhelming urge to follow Captain Action halfway across the globe that had motivated such a stunt in the boy. Maybe he was growing up.

He also realized then why the kid had paid so much attention to every detail of the mission. All the better to follow along covertly. The scope of his resourcefulness humbled the captain.

"She's in his hands, Sean. I'm not going to soft-pedal it. She's not well, and she needs our help. That's why you've got to listen to me from here on out and follow my every order to the letter. Uliana's life might depend upon it."

"Geez," grumbled the boy, unable to look Drake in the face. "I really fouled things up, huh?"

"Sean, how did you get here? From the camp, I mean."

"The Snow Streak, Cap," he said plainly, as if he wondered why he'd be asked such a dumb question.

The captain ran a hand through his hair, glanced up at the valleymen gathered around the pair, eyes wide in wonder and confusion.

"The Snow…? Okay, never mind that now. But, don't you see? You've provided us a way *out* of here, Sean. I couldn't ask for anything better."

Brightened, Sean Barrett asked what was next for them.

"First," said Captain Action, "we'll need Bury here to get us out of the City and back to the prisoner area…and quick. Our friend the doctor's going to be making an appearance again soon, and I need to be ready for him."

"Oh!" yelped the young man and suddenly dug into his backpack. Pulling out an object wrapped in a thick, soft cloth, he unwrapped it and tossed to his mentor.

"Here ya go, Cap, a little bit of home here in Tunguska. Thought you might miss it…"

Drake caught the object and stared at it. His hat. The real deal.

"C'mon, Sean," he said as he set it on his head with one smooth motion.

"We haven't one moment to lose…"

XIV
EVIL

Miles Drake often found that when things started to happen around him, really started clicking, they created a momentum all their own that speeded them along to their conclusion.

Of course, inevitably, there were always a few obstacles along the way.

"You have much to answer for," growled the Russian lieutenant called Flins as he stabbed a finger at Captain Action. "And you *will* answer for it all. Once we are gone from this place, I will…"

"Put a sock in it," retorted the captain as he walked away from the livid lieutenant. He was *thinking* now, his mind racing to conclusions and he didn't need any Russian road blocks to slow him down. Maybe the hat was helping him think; it wouldn't surprise him a bit.

From somewhere out of the darkness of the prisoner area, Juthrbog flitted to his side and leaned in to whisper in his ear.

"He is causing trouble. He will not be silenced and will get us all killed."

Thank goodness that Sean had remained in the City, thought Drake. One more impediment to action he didn't need. Not now.

"Listen," he told the albino, "Flins will have to just cry to himself. Nothing can be done about guys like that. When things start happening, look out for yourself and any of the men who you feel you can trust. The rest will just have to follow our lead."

Juthrbog stared at him with his dead eyes. "You have a plan?"

Drake nodded, more to himself than anything, then looked around the chamber and focused on the raging Flins. "Yes, yes I do. Now, I most certainly do."

He walked headlong across the area, making a beeline for the great and powerful "god of death." The man had his back turned as he strode up to him, but the captain reached out and spun him around by the shoulder.

And then laid a stunning punch right on Death's jaw.

Juthrbog rushed up to him. "I thought you said you had a plan!"

Drake smiled grimly, rubbing his hand. "*That's* my plan."

Eight valleymen were needed to break apart the combatants. It took almost all of them to drag Captain Action down the rocky corridor, at the direction of one of the engineers.

If everything was going according to plan, thought Drake, he'd be off to see the wizard.

As the cortège neared the grand audience chamber, and the engineer who led them disappeared around a corner ahead, the captain whirled into action.

Being able to think more clearly and finding a bit of time in the City to work out some of the kinks in his muscles lent steam to his purpose. He never actually relished violence, but, at the moment, cracking a few heads seemed just the thing to make him feel alive again.

Now if he could just put down six or more of the dwellers before the cyclops came back to see what was the matter, things might just work out.

Grabbing the arm of the nearest guard, he swung the man around and slammed him into two others; they all went down hard in a jumble of limbs. From inside his hat, the captain pulled out a small plastic disc which he broke open and then smashed on the floor of the cavern with one mighty throw.

Lightning exploded in the darkness. He'd closed his eyes, anticipating the burst, but for the unaware valleymen who's spent their lives in the underground it was as if the ceilings had opened up and the sun came down to play.

He laid out a few more with well-placed blows. Then something whooshed past his ear and he turned just in time to avoid another swing of a sickle-blade at his neck. Drake caught the only partially-blinded valleyman by his knife arm and pushed the man's fist directly into his own face. The man grunted, dropped the blade and then dropped to the ground himself.

Captain Action turned suddenly, crouched, and reached for the sickle-knife. Up ahead, the engineer came back around the corner, his single, monstrous eye taking in the entire scene.

From under the brim of his hat, Drake pulled down a pair of goggles. Thin and ultra-compact, the protective lenses slipped easily over his eyes. With three more of the discs from his hat in hand, he rushed at the engineer.

The blade he threw stuck in the man's eye port. Then he pitched another disc directly at the grotesque helmet. It went off with a blinding flash as it struck the skull-shaped helmet dead-on.

Captain Action leapt into the air and placed a roundhouse kick into the engineer's solar plexus, shattering his belt with a loud snap. Instantaneously gas started pouring from devices on the broken waist strap.

Plugs from his hat band went directly into his nostrils. He then waded into the gas and delivered a jabbing series of devastating blows to the suited figure.

Stepping over the crumpled form of the engineer, Captain Action glanced back at his handiwork and then turned to run down the corridor and towards his date with destiny.

Thankfully, he ran into no more engineers along his path. Something was up, obviously, and he guessed it was all wrapped up with the interruption to the earlier "address" in the City.

Whatever it was, he knew the clock was ticking away and he'd little time to ponder it.

The captain flew up and onto the giant platform and to the huts atop it. There he found the door to the doctor's hut locked.

"There's never a lightning sword around when you need one," he grumbled under his breath, hoping he'd be able to retrieve the weapon from wherever it'd been stashed after his latest capture. For now, he'd have to find another way of breaching the door.

Drake stood back from the metal obstacle, sized it up, and then planted a solid blow with his boot to its lock.

The door crumpled a bit then sprung open.

"Well, that works, too, obviously," he said in surprise and stepped inside the darkened hut, wary of ambushes.

The room inside was empty of any other human beings. Or doctors, for that matter.

Uliana Ulanova was nowhere to be seen.

A niggling tickle of frustration crawled up Captain Action's spine as he raced around the room, searching for signs of the woman. Within thirty seconds he had it completely torn apart.

In a way, the act of destruction felt good. And he found his sword.

Sheathing the weapon, Drake then turned to look at the other doorway in the room. A ghost of a breeze blew in from the rocky corridor that extended from the opening, slanting downwards into shadows. If he opened his ears to their fullest, he could swear he heard voices from somewhere down in the darkness.

He drew one good breath and raced into the gap and down into the unknown.

He found an ancient stairway that began a short distance into the corridor. Reaching up under the brim of his cap once more, he slipped another wafer-thin set of lenses in place over the others he wore. Night became day to his sight as the world around him was lit up with a soft reddish glow.

Seeing the staircase more clearly, the captain descended.

Finally, he came off the stairs and onto a level place. Ahead of him, a large doorway opened out onto a kind of terrace or balcony.

There, upon that ledge, stood Dr. Ling and one of his engineers.

Captain Action could see he was too late to stop the man from returning to "address" the City people. With the monstrous eye once more in his hands, the doctor was already deep into another act of obscene human subjugation.

Which also meant that he was in a state which could only be described as a trance.

The engineer stood back a few feet from his master, broadcasting his translated speech. The captain took in the arrangement, made decisions. He needed to act and act immediately; there'd never be a better opportunity.

He dove at the engineer and caught him around the legs with his arms. The suited figure, caught unaware, toppled over and crashed against the balcony's heavy stone railing. Drake could hear a few gasps and other vocalizations from the crowd below.

Swiftly he sprung to his feet and turned his attention to the doctor. The man continued in his attempt at mind control, unaware of Captain Action's entry. The state in which he'd plunged his own mind to control others' was apparently deep and all-consuming.

I could kill him, right here, right now, thought Drake. *I'd be doing the world a favor,* he reasoned to himself.

But it just wasn't his way. He'd have to stop the man in a different fashion.

As he reached for the doctor, a stabbing pain in his thigh screamed for his attention. He looked down to see a hypodermic needle sticking out of his leg and the fallen engineer reeling back to view the results of his handiwork.

Drake kicked out by reflex, a protective movement. He caught the suited figure in the chest, sending the man sprawling backwards and over the railing.

"No!" he yelled in disbelief and flung himself to the railing to peer over its edge. There, far below, lay the ragdoll form of the engineer.

The captain whipped back around, beginning to feel the effects of the narcotic, and glared at the doctor. Pulling the needle from his leg and throwing it to the side, he advanced on the man and knocked the hideous eye device from his hands. The doctor didn't even blink.

Stepping behind his foe, Captain Action reached out with both hands and dug his fingers viciously into the man's collar. Then, with one quick action, he tore the rubbery mask from his head, exposing him to the dwellers below.

If evil had a face, it was exemplified by that which sprung from underneath the mask.

Gigantic, lidless white eyes extended from a bony skull covered in a sickly blue-tinged sheath of skin. Jagged, uneven teeth rested in a mouth that twisted into a devilish grin. The satanic motif continued in the form of almost gracefully pointed ears. Veins, large and bloated, throbbed in azure temples.

But the features below the man's temples paled in comparison to what rested above them. There sat a visible brain, angry and pulsating in its bony cradle. The twisting rivulets of the organ's matter were red-tinged and grotesquely veined; a stark sight which defied explanation of its surreality.

What the man was, Captain Action could not say for sure. Of how he functioned as a living, breathing entity, he was perhaps even more unsure. If he was an alien organism, not of this Earth, that too was up for debate. The A.C.T.I.O.N. Directorate's sole purpose was to identify and defend from extraterrestrial invaders, but even that organization had thus far failed in determining the origins of the obscene creature known as Dr. Evil.

All Miles Drake knew was that the man had once existed as a human being, or so he believed, and that he'd somehow and for some reason given up that existence for a mission of pure evil.

And that he'd killed Sean Barrett's parents at their compound in Argentina.

For now, Captain Action stepped back from his sworn enemy and gifted the evil creature to his admiring fans below in the City.

Dr. Evil's eyes fluttered as some telltale synapses in his exposed brain seemed to inform him that things had changed.

Coming back to full cognizance, he looked down from the balcony and into the hundreds of faces that looked back up at him.

Faces filled with shock. Faces filled with disgust. Faces filled with abject loathing.

Then, rebellion.

XV
RECOVERY

"Cap, wake up!"

Miles Drake opened his eyes to find Sean leaning over him, shaking him. Realization and awareness flooded into him, spread through his body. He sat up and was awarded with dizziness. His mouth tasted like he imagined dirty socks might taste.

"C'mon," implored the boy. "There's still fighting."

He found he'd been unconscious for only a short time, barely a half-cycle according to Bury. The dweller tried to keep pace with the captain as the A.C.T.I.O.N. agent followed Sean through the darkened passageways of the underground realm, filling him in on recent developments.

"We're taking back our home," said Bury plainly. "Bring is directing the movements of our kinsmen. We've already made some progress. The Forbidden is once again sealed and the mining has been stopped. Our ceremonial blades no longer draw blood."

"Where is Dr. Evil?" asked Drake, checking his belt and sword for the tenth time and adjusting his hat for the eleventh.

"Locked away."

"Where?"

"I can't tell you that, Miles, but believe me when I say that he's been secured. He's not a danger to us anymore."

The captain stopped walking and skewered the valleyman with a look.

"Evil is always a danger. Secured, locked up, key tossed away; that fiend is always going to be dangerous."

They rounded a bend in the passageway and came out into the Gardens. Dwellers milled about, checking the foliage and talking in low tones among themselves. Some turned to look at the captain and his youthful companion and grimaced.

"I can promise you and the boy safe passage," said Bury, "but only for as long as it will take you to leave. The collective desire is to have you and your companions *gone*. We have been at peace for thousands of turn-cycles until that man came here."

"The others aren't my companions," Drake told him without emotion. "But, yes, we all need to leave. I understand that. But, there is one, a woman, who still needs to be found. And I'm going to find her."

The valleyman looked throughtful. "Perhaps she's with the...what do you call them? Soldiers?"

He translated that for Sean, who'd been picking up bits and pieces of the conversation, getting the gist of it.

"I checked, Cap," offered Sean. "The Russians are holed up in the prison area. They've plugged up the way in and are attacking anybody who gets close to 'em. But I'm pretty sure Yu-Yu's not with them."

Drake wondered about Juthrbog, about where his loyalties would lie when the chips were down and things got dicey.

"And the engineers?"

"The Eyes," replied Bury, "are trapped in their metal caves, much like the soldiers."

"Then," said Captain Action grimly, "it's a two-front war, I guess."

Drake peered around an outcropping of rock to get a view of the platform in the audience chamber. For his sins, he was blown backwards by a small, sharp explosion not ten feet in front of him.

Dusting himself off, he looked up at Sean and Bury with a glum expression on his face.

"Well, they're not being very sociable, that's for sure."

The young man paced around, his agitation palpable. "But it's just *five* of those freaks, right? You said so yourself, Cap, we can rock-n-sock 'em easy!"

"No," Bury hissed when the captain translated. "Not all of our kinsmen are Free again. Some of them remain Taken and in the service of the Eyes. The servants of Evil are not alone in those chambers. Some of my people are fighting *with* them."

Captain Action flipped several lenses onto and off of his eyes, staring all the while at the huts on the platform, making sure to stay low and not make himself a target again for the engineers' weapons.

Finally, he expressed satisfaction with a grunt and flipped the thin goggles back up into his hat brim.

"Heat signatures are concentrated in the farthest structure but there are just two of them in the second from the left."

"You think they have her there, Cap?" trilled Sean, hope rising in his young face.

"That's what I'm going to find out, pal."

At Bury's direction and with Bring's approval, Captain Action was given a large shroud of the woven black material that the dwellers used ubiquitously. He draped it over himself and motioned for the odd lights to be dimmed and then fully extinguished.

Blacked-out, both the chamber and himself, he crawled out into the open, then got up into a low crouch and crab-ran across the rocky floor.

Almost immediately small arms fire erupted around him.

Drake wasn't kidding himself that he could completely fool the monitoring devices the engineers possessed both in their helmets and in the huts, but he damn well felt he could at least confuse them a little. He serpentined towards the platform's long set of stairs, swiftly and silently to the accompaniment of a symphony of death.

He'd just about reached the bottommost step when the entire staircase lit up with a burst and then crumpled and fell. It crashed to the floor below with a deafening cacophony.

Well, he winced; that was to be expected.

Shucking the shroud, Captain Action tore off in a full run towards the support structure of the platform and got himself underneath it within seconds. He desperately hoped it would provide him some cover to make his way to its upper reaches.

Like an ape in the jungle, Drake leapt and grabbed at the poles of the web-like structure, swinging from them and making his way slowly and surely upward. Bursts of gunfire continued; he surmised that his opponents believed that the valleymen would come charging in next.

But he was alone in this particular mission. If he were to rescue Uliana neatly and efficiently, he couldn't afford any other soul to look after. Sean Barrett had been warned in no uncertain terms that accompanying his mentor this time was not an option.

As if that trick ever worked on the boy before, he thought to himself with a sigh.

Reaching the underside of the platform, the captain broke and then tossed more of the plastic discs from his hat up and onto its surface. They went off with resounding booms and bright flashes. Then he swung up and over, stood up and unsheathed his lightning sword.

The hut he suspected the woman to occupy was nearest to him, but the one in which the small army hid was more of a concern to him at the moment. Drake knew he needed to somehow, at all costs, cut off the possibility of engagement with that army.

As he thought of them, the door to the far hut was flung open and several valleymen poured out into the open. Seeing the A.C.T.I.O.N. agent, they charged down the platform in his direction, brandishing their sickle-blades.

Captain Action whipped around and struck out with his sword. Cutting into the hinges of the door of the nearest hut, he scooped up the large metal portal and brandished it like a horizontal shield.

Then, taking a deep breath, he let out a war cry and ran towards the oncoming valleymen.

Using the door, the captain slammed headlong into the attackers, bowling them over like a game of tenpins. He expertly twirled in place, bashing any stragglers into oblivion, and then took out the very last of his explosive discs. Breaking it open, he tossed it into the open door of the hut from which the dwellers had exited.

The disc caught an emerging engineer at point-blank range; the resulting burst sent the man sprawling. Without hesitation, Drake slammed the door closed and then used his own portal to wedge it shut. Feeling it was secure, he turned and sprinted back to the first metal house, praying that Uliana was safe inside it and without further injury.

Arriving at the darkened doorframe, he looked inside, his heart pounding in his breast. He was fully unprepared for the sight that greeted him there.

Uliana Ulanova, dressed only in the torn upper half of an engineer's suit with her shockingly golden tresses loose and wild, stood with bare legs akimbo over the prone and bare-chested form of one of Dr. Evil's henchmen.

Her face sprung upwards with a snap at Drake's arrival, her brown eyes flashing with savage violence. In her hand she gripped a metal pole, one end of which was bloodied and bent.

Her eyes softened only slightly when she finally recognized him, realized he was alive.

"What took you so long, Captain?"

XVI
STORY

It was her! It was really her.

The Sixty-Fifth Bury looked upon her and wondered why he wasn't happier. It had been so long. Shouldn't he be glad? But, sadly, her presence only furthered the onrushing splintering of his kinsmen.

Where once New Lake was One, now it was separating into chambers, enclaves of opinion that threatened to divide them forever. He wanted to be happy over the sight of her, but a small voice in the back of his head told him that she'd bring little light to the darkness that now prevailed.

Removing Evil was an important step, he thought. And, unfortunately, removing the others would be just as important. The caverns must be cleared so that the people could be One again. He'd move rock and stone to see that happen.

But it was good to see her again.

Coming down from her captivity on the platform and going out among the dwellers, Uliana had caused quite a stir. Drake had never seen such a phenomenon; the valleymen were mesmerized.

Heck, he admitted to himself; *he* was mesmerized.

Then tensions flared. He could feel it in the warm air of the underground realm, an almost physical division that was splitting the once united people into camps. Some wanted every single "visitor" gone, while others had begun to ponder thoughts of opening channels of exchange with the outside world. Still others, he saw with dread, were thinking thoughts of violence.

As a stranger in a strange land, Captain Action had to be ready for anything, at any time. While he gathered up all the soldiers to leave, he felt exposed and vulnerable, two feelings he hated more than anything else.

Thankfully Uliana seemed well, or at least as well as one could be after what she'd been put through. Drake hung back, giving her room to process the situation naturally, before he began to ask her the questions that had been burning in his head for weeks on end. He watched her and he waited.

Sean was antsy, but that was to be expected in a thirteen-year-old. The young man was overjoyed to see Uliana again, and the captain decided to not pull Sean back; it seemed as if his exuberance might actually be good for her. Overall, though, she'd changed since the ordeal. Drake couldn't quite put his finger on it, but she held herself differently and he wondered if it was the environment or, perhaps, the people around her that fed the change. Regardless, he wondered what the future held for her.

Bury was almost perpetually worried now. He'd told Captain Action of his growing concerns and of the flames that were being stoked in the hearts of his fellows. Their continued presence was a firebrand, he said, one that the valleyman feared.

Overall, Drake chafed at the inaction that followed Uliana's liberation, but, in the absence of activity, he believed he might still make some headway into the problems that festered all around him.

"You have questions," she said, sitting cross-legged on the floor of a small chamber near the Gardens, one she'd been "magnanimously" afforded by the dwellers. They seemed to want to keep a distance between her and the City.

"Yeah," said the captain, sighing. "Yeah, I won't lie to you. I've got a ton of them. Are you ready to provide some answers?"

The woman looked down into her lap, said nothing. She was dressed in the garb of the valleymen and Drake thought it suited her despite her lustrous, shining gold hair. *That* was something that would never fit in among the strange world below the surface.

"And, by the way, I knew you were wearing a wig all along," he told her, grinning. When she gave him a look of disbelief, he cocked a thumb at himself.

"Hey, 'master of disguise,' remember?"

"Yes," she said finally, looking back up at him with the loveliest eyes he'd ever had the pleasure of swimming in. "I will tell you the story, but I think we should do something about the heavy air that sits upon our shoulders. *Everyone's* shoulders."

"How do you propose we do that?"

She smiled, a small sad thing. "We remove two of the biggest worries from their minds, at least for a short while."

And with that, she stood up and reached out to take his hand.

Soon they stood over the opening to a shaft in the rock that plunged downward into utter darkness. In the soft illumination from Uliana's light-stick, Captain Action could see that the uneven walls of the shaft might *just* be able to provide hand-and footholds for someone to climb down provided he could see what he was doing.

Somewhere far below, he could swear he heard running water. It was also cooler in the area in which they stood, but his uniform provided him with the insulation he'd need. Uliana wore only the dark suit of the valleymen's woven material, but had removed her fur boots and leggings and now carried a small pack on her back and a rough-hewn flask on her belt.

Drake asked what was at the bottom of the drop.

"The story," she told him. "Though I will begin it as we climb down."

"I worry that we don't have time for this," the captain said, staring into the shaft.

"But its part of the story, what lies below..."

"Still, I worry."

Uliana knelt, swung her legs over the side of the opening, then began to find her footholds and descend.

"You will find that time seems immutable here in this place," she reassured him, looking up to make sure he was following her.

The captain mirrored her actions, climbing down into the hole, watching her, taking in her sure movements, her hair, her lithe body.

"Uliana, you haven't just been here before. You're *from* here, aren't you?"

"I learned from Bury," her voice spoke from below, quite obviously trying to change the subject, "that Bring will attempt to parlay with Flins and Marowit and the rest."

She paused in her descent. "But yet my people will not speak to me."

"Why?" he asked, realizing she'd just answered his question.

The woman looked up at him, found his eyes with her own in the wan light. "Because of this." She indicated her golden hair.

"But it's *beautiful*," he said as they began to move again.

"Thank you, Captain." Drake could almost hear her smile in the darkness, or maybe it was just that he saw it in his mind's eye.

"There was a time," she continued, "when I was completely, utterly ashamed of it.

"Being born different," Uliana said as she fingered an outcropping, "can either be something to define a person for the good, or haunt her forever. I was born with golden hair, not brown or gray, and no one, no one at all in the entirety of New Lake, had ever seen anything like it in his lifetime. And it disturbed them.

Captain Action could see that the uneven walls of the shaft might just be able to provide hand- and footholds for someone to climb down.

"At first my parents thought it a gift, until an old man among us, the most ancient of my kinsmen at the time, named Count, took a disliking to me. Can you imagine? Only a few years old and I was already hated. You see, Count liked very much his position as, well, you would say a shaman, but that isn't really correct. But, for lack of better term, let us just say that.

"Count told others that I was a bad omen, a sure sign of ghosts from our shared past that sought to bring devilment upon the City. He himself bedeviled me, at every turn, and for years. To make a long story short, he then had me exiled."

Captain Action's face flushed from anger over Uliana's past predicament and his sudden distraction cost him a foothold. He scrabbled at the wall of the shaft with one boot, but only managed to kick loose a small rain of pebbles and stones.

Then Uliana reached up and caught his foot with her hand. Giving him the footing he needed to regain his composure, he then managed to find a new place to set his boot.

They continued downward.

"Father went with me, said he could not leave me, all of twelve years old, to the outside world. He did not know that I had been sneaking out from our caverns on a regular basis and spying on, sometimes even interacting with, the Evenks in the region. And the Russians. I loved my home, but the Above called to me.

"Together we made our way to Chelyabinsk and there we made a home. Father created new names for us and we tried to forget all about New Lake.

"Then when I was sixteen, I left Chelyabinsk for Moscow. By myself. To educate myself and find a cure for what was killing Father and myself, also."

"But the radiation," he said, getting the knack of finding the right spots to place his hands and feet. "The men who attacked Directorate headquarters; they died. And they couldn't have been gone from here for more than a month or so?"

"I'm coming to that," Uliana replied. "I studied radiation at the universities and earned my degree on the subject. I hoped to learn enough about my people's curse to, well, to come back and have something to offer them. To make it so they wouldn't hate me, be afraid of me. I suppose that was a very childish outlook on things."

Drake looked down at her. "No, not at all. It was honorable. You wanted to do what was right for them."

The woman reached a level spot at the bottom of the shaft and she held her light-stick up higher to allow him an easier time of the final drop. Then, when they stood together, he turned to her.

"The two people you said you took readings off of? A man and a woman? You and your father, I assume?"

"Someone has his thinking cap on," she said taking him in with her gaze, running her eyes across his face, his uniform. "Yes, that's so, but Father died just last year, in Chelyabinsk."

Drake furrowed his brow. "He couldn't have been too old?"

Uliana looked away. "No, he died of the radiation, like the men sent to kill you. He died so that I would live and continue my work."

Captain Action followed her gaze and saw what she was looking at. In the glow from her illumination, he saw an underground grotto before them.

The small space was low-ceilinged and not very wide, a pocket in the earth lined with a jumble of rocks and boulders. Off to one side, a minute stream of water ran down from between two stones and into a tiny pool in the middle of the grotto. The air held the smell of minerals, but not unpleasantly so.

He tried not to think of how deep they were, how far below the city, how even farther below the surface of the earth. In the faint light, the stream and the pool were a quaint sight, making him almost forget the unfathomable tons of rock and soil that hung above his head.

"I came here as a little girl quite often," Uliana told him as she stepped towards the center of the space. "When I wasn't traipsing around Above.

"Down here no one had to look at me."

Drake found his way over to the water, knelt down to look at it more closely. "This is what you brought me here to see."

She knelt down beside him, brushing up against his thigh and arm with her own.

"Yes, Captain. I discovered that the water holds *something*, a mineral, an element, something that *masks* the radiation in our bodies, holds it at bay. I distilled it into a powder and took it with us when my Father and I left the City. And we ingested it as capsules, once every six months or so. And we lived, like my kinsmen lived here under the ground."

"And no one else knows of it?"

"No," she said quietly, not looking at him, but staring down into the pool. "No one. Here, in our world, no one needed to know, I reasoned. The substance, whatever it is, is in the very air here. Perhaps you saw the mist over New Lake? And here, in this stream, this pool, it's in its most concentrated form."

Captain Action stood up, carefully, so as not to bump his head against the stone ceiling. She stood, too, facing him, but remained silent.

"Uliana, now that we've finally gotten to the, ahh, bottom of it all," he glanced around him, "why didn't you just tell me this before?"

A hard look came into her face but then softened after a moment.

"I was fixated on returning here, to the detriment of all else; I admit it. I defected to the United States in hope of finding better research facilities, but the pills were almost gone, I could feel myself getting ill. You only saw the glow from my radiation before because of the shielding that's apparently around that hut."

She reached out and traced his chin, his mouth with her finger, slowly.

"And, then, I didn't want to tell you because I didn't want you to find cause to reject me."

A light came into his eyes, along with realization. He saw her backpack more clearly then, the rolled-up mat of soft material within.

"Uliana, I don't know what to say…"

Her finger came to rest, centered over his lips.

"Then say nothing."

She leaned into him, but he met her eagerly halfway.

In an oubliette somewhere beneath the hidden city of New Lake squatted the strange being called Dr. Evil. Though dethroned and imprisoned, he remained in good spirits.

Thoughts flashed through his exposed brain. Electrical impulses hurdled through the nooks and crannies of its evil matter, a virtual storm of plans and schemes.

The man did not consider himself beaten. He reflected upon his current situation and labeled it as temporary, a way station after which he'd soon continue his work. And, if possible, have his revenge.

Dr. Evil leaned forward in the darkness and put his index fingers against his temples and his thumbs just below his pointed ears. Then he closed his eyes.

Several minutes elapsed before he stirred from his apparent somnambulism. He did not remove his digits from his skull, but a low hum issued forth from his mouth.

He began to send his thoughts out into the ether. Evil and twisted, if they were a tangible thing on the physical plane, they might have appeared as tongues of fire or even bolts of lightning.

He sought out an individual, a particular figure in close proximity to his own mortal body. After several long minutes that stretched out to just under a half hour, Dr. Evil made contact with the individual.

Then he began to make a few suggestions.

Miles Drake offered his hand to his beautiful companion and helped her up and out of the rocky shaft. She pulled herself up and purposefully pressed against the captain as she stood and dusted off her garments.

"Uliana, you had said you were also trying to look into the origins of your home," he inquired as they began to walk away from the secret place, hand in hand. "What do you know of it?"

She hung her head down and her golden locks fell all about her face. "Only that my people came more than a thousand years ago from some other place. They were fleeing something, some sort of tyranny or oppression, and somehow found their way *here*."

"I have some ideas on that 'other place,'" he told her. "What else do you know?"

"Very little, save that we, over the centuries, have taken in others, from the outside, to deepen the gene pool?" She gave his hand a small squeeze.

Before Drake could respond in kind, they arrived at the spot in the Gardens where they were scheduled to meet Bury and to retrieve Sean. The valleyman was there alone.

"Where's Sean?" asked Captain Action, instantly on alert and releasing Uliana's hand.

Bury looked down sheepishly and took a step back. The spot he vacated was suddenly filled by several figures.

In the lead came Flins. Behind him were several of the Russian soldiers, a few valleymen and Bring.

"So good of you to return, Comrade," said the Soviet lieutenant with a smug grin. It looked as if the simple act of smiling might crack his entire homely face.

Uliana leapt forward, into Flins' path. "Where is the boy?" she said from between gritted teeth.

The lieutenant's hand shot out and struck her soundly across the face. The blow sent Uliana straight to the ground.

Captain Action let out an inarticulate growl of rage and swung at the Russian, only to find several sets of hands grabbing at him and pulling him back.

Bring spat commands to his valleymen to hold the outsider tightly.

Then he turned to Flins, as if to listen to what the man had to say.

"We don't fully comprehend the language, you see," said the lieutenant, indicating the valleymen, "but we understand it enough to have made a pact with our new comrades here."

"You are under arrest, Captain," he said, reaching for the lightning sword, "as an 'undesirable' agent of a foreign power."

XVII
SENTENCE

In one of the highest structures in New Lake, a tribunal was called into being. The dwellers below the Earth had never been witness to such a thing nor ever had any need for one. It was a foreign concept to them and, to some among the dwellers below, it was not entirely welcome.

"I don't care for this," announced the Sixty-Fifth Bury. "I'm not so sure I even fully comprehend it."

His wrists bound securely in front of him, Captain Action stood tall next to him as they waited in a small room just outside the hastily arranged tribunal chamber. Sean Barrett was not with them, but the captain was assured that he was safe and not being mistreated.

"It must be the Soviets' idea. They love things like this for all their talk of equality among the masses and the common good; they never miss a chance to push people around."

"But," said Bury, "a-a body that presides over others? Institutes strictures that may affect another's life or well-being? It's an abomination…"

Drake was reminded of Uliana's mention of her ancestors fleeing from tyranny or some such; he could see how the roots of Bury's distaste for a court of justice ran deep and wide.

Before he could comment further, the room took a sudden chill. Turning slightly, he watched as the other prisoner was brought in for his sentencing.

Dr. Evil was being led, also bound at the wrists, by two Russian soldiers. Valleymen accompanied them, too, but gave the doctor a wide berth; their disgust over the man was palpable. The captain was just grateful that Sean wasn't present with his parents' murderer.

Bury scowled at his kinsmen and then walked up to them.

"Never would I have believed that such a day would arrive," he spat at them. "I'm appalled at our participation in this travesty."

Evil perked up at that, grinned devilishly.

"Never fear, my friends," he said aloud, in Russian. "This will all be over shortly and fairly neatly.

◆ ◆ ◆

Outside the city, in the outer chambers, Dr. Evil's engineers still held their ground on the platform in the audience chamber. They'd grown quiet, holed-up in a few of the metal huts, and had not recently shown their helmeted faces.

Word of this came to Captain Action, and he wondered what the blue-skinned devil's henchmen were up to. Nothing good, he mused to himself.

Inside the tribunal chamber, Evil himself held his ground and listened laconically to the words from the long table that sat at the head of the room. Flins was speaking. Alongside him sat Bring, a few others of his kinsmen, and Marowit.

"After much deliberation among the people of the City and their Russian friends," he made a gesture to indicate himself, "a sentence has been passed on the alien that stands before us now."

"If I may speak on my behalf?" inquired the prisoner. Drake perked up, puzzled at the turn of events.

The valleymen were visibly disturbed by the request. Flins looked down the table at his fellow lieutenant, Marowit. The thin man looked even more emaciated than normal, obviously still suffering from the wounds he took in the battle of the encampment. He nodded weakly at Flins, who in turn gave a curt nod of his head to the prisoner.

"All I care to say," Dr. Evil noted in Russian, "was that I have great respect for this body and I trust they will do the right thing."

"Then you will feel comforted," said Flins, "as we pronounce you guilty of all charges and sentence you to die in what our friends here refer to as the Swamp."

Bury reacted strongly to the announcement when Captain Action whispered a translation to him. He sprang up suddenly, knocking over the stool on which he sat and then hurried out of the chamber with nary a comment.

Dr. Evil stood silently, malevolence swirling about him stemming from his smug smile; he seemed completely unfazed by the sentence.

"I'd like to speak, also, if that's not too much of an imposition."

Flins' dark eyes clouded with menace as he turned to the speaker. "The room recognizes Captain Action."

Drake cut right to it, without preamble. "Myself, the boy, and this man," he indicated the doctor, "are wholly of the outside world, the Above." He spoke in the language of the valleymen, or the closest approximation he could muster at that moment. The Russians frowned at this and leaned in to attempt to decipher the captain's words on the spot.

"We need to return to that world. I will remove us from here, your City, and never return. If you will allow me, I will see to it that Dr. Evil stands before a body such as this in my country and be tried according to the laws of my people.

"This I swear to you."

Flins whipped his head back and forth, searching the faces of his valleymen compatriots, unsure of what he had just heard. Then he demanded a translation.

"I told them I'd take the doctor here back to the States and see that he's brought to justice, Lieutenant." Captain Action took a step forward. "You and I both know that would be the right thing to do. And you and your men need to leave, too. This isn't our place and we have no right to be here, messing around like this."

Dr. Evil also stepped forward, coming almost shoulder-to-shoulder with his nemesis. He addressed Flins.

"Are you going to sit there and listen to this, Comrade?" he said darkly. "You will take orders from this peacock?"

"Be quiet!" bellowed Flins. "Both of you!"

Suddenly and violently, the door to the room was flung open and Uliana Ulanova strode in.

She was dressed in a more elaborate version of the normal clothes of the dwellers, with embroidered sashes and a garment that looked like a skirt or a kilt sitting rakishly on her hips. Her golden tresses had been combed out and appeared as if a halo around her lovely face, which had been accentuated with mineral dust around her eyes, her high cheekbones, and her lips.

The valleymen in the room became apoplectic at her entrance. Bury came in behind her and smiled to himself at the reaction to her presence.

The Russians sat there, jaws hanging open, eyes wide with wonder.

"I do not *ask* to speak," said the woman in the language of her kinsmen, "for that is not our way. We speak if we have something to say, and our words are always held in great respect by our fellows. I *will* speak now!"

The chamber devolved into chaos. Bring stood up and moved as if to leap over the table at Uliana. Captain Action tensed, ready to protect her despite being bound although he suspected she could handle herself without his help.

Confirmation came through on that account before he could barely finish his thought.

"Outrage!" screamed Bring. "In the name of my grandsire Count, I cast you out once more!"

And with that he charged on Uliana.

Drake cut him off in mid-run. He slammed into the valleyman full force with his body and together they went sprawling into the table, shattering it. Somewhere behind him, he heard a cry of fury and then realized it had come from Uliana.

Violence spread across the chamber, seizing everyone present in its grip, save Dr. Evil. He stood back and licked his lips as he viewed the melee.

Captain Action suddenly found his hands free. Bury jumped back and quickly hid a sickle-blade beneath his garments. Drake got up, hauled Bring to his feet and landed a roundhouse punch on the man's jaw. Then he turned his attention to Flins.

The Russian stood still, covering the A.C.T.I.O.N. agent with a submachine gun.

"From one of Dr. Evil's own caches of weapons, Comrade. You will cease this disturbance immediately."

The fight was, apparently, over before it had barely begun.

Wrists again bound securely, but this time behind his back, Drake stood before the tribunal once more. Uliana had been forcibly ejected from the chamber, Bury with her. He was alone.

"We actually understand your reluctance to accept our decisions, Captain," said Flins, glancing over to Bring, who glowered and rubbed his jaw. "But you are in no position to dictate what we will or will not do here with prisoners."

He then motioned to the soldiers who had brought Drake into the room.

"Take him away. He'll be brought back in after our deliberations on his *own* case now."

"This is bad," said Uliana, applying a salve to his shoulder.

"No, no, it's not," Sean Barrett insisted. "We can still get out of here. Can't we, Cap?"

Drake was deep in thought. He'd been brought back out to the small area that Uliana was occupying, still a prisoner and still under guard. The situation, he had to admit, *was* pretty bad.

There seemed to be three factions forming. One was Flins, Marowit, and the majority of the soldiers still loyal to the Soviet cause and their lieutenants. They were allied with a contingent of valleymen who, according to Bury, did not represent the true way of his kinsmen. They stood for change, a kind of change that threatened to destroy a thousand or more years of peace in the subterranean world.

Second was himself, Uliana, Sean, and Bury, who claimed that a good number of his people stood with him and they represented a Truth that needed to be preserved. If they could win the day, they would allow the outsiders to leave in peace and with a promise to never return. They would also let the captain take Dr. Evil with them.

This faction, he also believed, could rely on the support of Juthrbog and the rest of the soldiers. The lieutenant was walking a tightrope among his fellow Russians, but Drake was prepared to offer him and those loyal to him a safety net.

Then, third, was the remaining five engineers, their weapon-heavy fort and a handful of "taken" dwellers, somehow still in thrall to Dr. Evil. That faction remained a wild card.

"What is the Swamp?" he asked the woman, wincing from her application of the strong medicinal salve.

"A place of legends," she replied. "It lies beneath the City, the dwelling of monsters and of death. A tale told to children to get them to behave." She smiled ruefully at her words, memories playing at the edges of her thoughts.

"So, it's not real?" asked Sean, becoming very interested in the topic.

"No, it's a real thing, boy wonder, but, as far as I know, no one has gone into it for centuries. It was once used to discard the waste from the City, but we later found better ways to accomplish the same end. Still, going into the Swamp cannot be good; there *are* things there better left undisturbed."

Captain Action stood and began pulling his uniform shirt over his head. "I have no love for the doctor, but I can't stand by and let him be executed here. He needs to be taken back to the Directorate, interrogated, and then handed over to the authorities for trial."

"But," said Uliana, cocking her head to one side as she watched him dress, "then you would be doing almost exactly what my people are doing."

Drake looked at her quizzically.

"I do not pass judgment, Captain. I only point out…"

Bury rushed into the chamber, panting. "I just came from the City. You are ordered to return now to face the tribunal."

Sean handed his mentor his hat, then put his hand out. Drake took it in his, shook it firmly. Finally, he clapped the boy on the shoulder and told him to stay with Uliana and Bury.

"Captain!"

He turned to look into wet brown eyes, his face inscrutable.

Then after a moment, he turned to leave.

Dr. Evil and Captain Action stood again before the tribunal, a strange sight for anyone who knew their shared history. But no such person was present, so perhaps there was nothing strange to it, save for the captain's dynamic uniform and hat and the doctor's blue skin and exposed brain.

"This *creature*," said Flins, indicating Dr. Evil, "will be put into the Swamp. There he will meet his fate, whatever it shall be there."

The Soviet turned then to Captain Action.

"This man shall be put in with him. He, too, will meet his fate there, alongside his enemy.

"The woman and the boy will be ejected from the City, from the caverns, from this place entirely, without provisions or help of any kind. In the outside world, they will make their way or they will not."

Drake stood stunned. Next to him, his fellow prisoner began to chuckle under his breath, then proceeded to cackle in full voice.

His evil laugh filled the chamber to near bursting.

XVIII
ALLIANCES

Sean Barrett stood and watched the procession, feeling both helpless and useless. His hero and mentor, Captain Action, was being marched off to his death, alongside the man who had killed his mother and father.

The young man was granted permission to witness the good captain and the evil doctor ushered into the area called the Swamp; he took the offer with some small hope of spotting a way of freeing Miles Drake and, maybe, to strike some sort of blow against Dr. Evil.

That hope was crushed the moment Sean saw that the Russians and the valleymen had thoroughly covered their bases. He swiftly realized there'd be no rescue, no surprises, and no chance to turn the tables. Captain Action would soon disappear from his sight and his life forever.

He burned with youthful anger, hot and smoking. It wasn't fair, he thought to himself; heroes are supposed to survive their adventures! The bad guys were supposed to lose and go to jail! If only Captain Action were Superman or Batman.

No. No, he was who he was, Sean admitted to himself with shame. He was a good man who helped people and fought for his country and passed on his wisdom to bratty kids. If this was to be the end for him, well, he thought, it was a pretty darn good thing he was taking the bad guy with him.

Dr. Evil walked along, grinning, seemingly oblivious to his fate. Sean wanted to punch him in the face, stab him in the heart; do something to make him pay for his parents' deaths. He mused over that for a moment, then strode out and into the path of the procession.

The valleymen made a move to stop the boy, but Bring gestured for them to fall back. The dwellers below the earth had no real argument against Sean; in fact, some of them saw something in him that transcended his age. Perhaps they saw the making of a hero.

He stopped in front of Dr. Evil, then looked him up and down not with an expression of disgust, but one of dry pity.

"I am Sean Walsh Barrett," he told the doctor proudly. "And my mother and father live on through me. You didn't win then and you haven't won now."

Then he clapped his hands together and wiped them off on each other. He was done with Dr. Evil.

As he turned his back on the man and walked away, the doctor had lost his grin.

Captain Action swelled with pride; maybe he'd done all right by the kid after all.

Her feelings for Miles Benson Drake were a mess.

Uliana Ulanova paced the rough floor of her chamber, waiting for Sean to return from what she could only think of as an execution. Bury sat off to one side, watching her walk back and forth, shaking his head. *Let him*, she thought; *he thinks I've become too much like an outsider. Well*, she pondered, *perhaps I have.*

Who *was* she, exactly? Was she Brighten, the little girl with the golden hair who only wanted to be left alone and was summarily exiled for her "deformity"? Or was she Uliana, the woman who boldly conquered the halls of learning and delved deep into the tunnels of science? Or could she be only a tiny, scared thing who wanted to hide and deny any claim on any identity at all?

Captain Action had become a lightning rod in her life; of that one thing she was sure. But now he'd been taken away to his death by her kinsmen and she could do absolutely nothing about it. For all her heritage, for all her education, for all her experience at conquering adversity, she was completely helpless to save the man she…

Sean came in suddenly, rescuing her from her troubled thoughts. The boy, no, the young man, told her that Drake and Dr. Evil had been put into the Swamp and sealed away therein.

She wanted to hold Sean, offer him succor, but the change she now saw in him ran deep and she hesitated. Finally, he came into her arms and they held each other and thought about their friend.

Bury went out to leave them to their comforting of each other, then came back minutes later, telling Uliana that someone was just outside, waiting to see her.

It was Juthrbog and the little sergeant they called Skrzak.

"Of our original platoon," he told her in Russian, "there is roughly half the men left after the slaughter at the camp. Of those, eighteen are pledged to me and, in turn, now to you. We want to offer our aid in leaving this place. The sooner the better, for the men are chafing to be gone from the presence of the others, especially the lieutenants.

"They are no longer our countrymen."

Uliana stared into the man's eyes, looking for a sign of his sincerity. She'd seen far too many men with treachery in their souls; she didn't need one more. She and Sean now needed allies. They needed help before they were tossed, perhaps quite literally, to the wolves.

"What can I do for you?" she asked the albino, testing him. "I don't take without giving something in return."

Juthrbog, named for the god of the moon, rolled that question over in his own mind, chewing on its ramifications. Then he cleared his throat and spoke.

"Well, tsarina, quite frankly, we could use a leader. More than that, actually we could use a symbol."

"For what? I won't lead a rebellion against my own people, if that's what you have in mind."

The lieutenant glanced over at Bury, found support in the man's eyes, than looked back at the woman with the golden hair.

"To lead us in taking back what we have brought to this fantastic realm. Our taint. Our spore; the darkness with which we've saddled these people.

"Help us fight our fellow soldiers and give the valleymen back their world."

"They have promised that they will seize their own wayward people," interjected Bury, "clean out the nest of that evil man and then return to the Above. And hold the secret of our City within their hearts forever."

"You are the brother of my father," said Uliana to the man. "I trust you with my life. But I find it very difficult to trust *him* without reservation. He was involved. He helped torture the captain."

The albino stiffened, drew himself up in soldierly fashion. "I am not proud of my actions, tsarina. I will carry my sins with me for the rest of my life, but I cannot seek to correct *all* of them *here*, under the earth. Only the ones at hand. I and my men want to fight *now* for what we can, *then* take our chances back in the motherland."

"I need a sign from you," said Uliana, fixing the man with a cold, hard look. "I need a symbol of your intent."

The lieutenant nodded curtly, then motioned for Skrzak to come forward. The little sergeant stepped up, holding something wrapped in cloth. Carefully, he opened the bundle and showed its contents to the woman.

It was Captain Action's lightning sword.

"Will this do?" asked the albino.

The surly Russian called Flins arrived outside the beautiful woman's chamber just in time to meet his fellow lieutenant and the company clerk on their way out. This made the man very unhappy and he told them so.

"I go where I wish to go," said Juthrbog stiffly. "Now that we have conquered Evil, I think we have the run of this place, *da*, Comrade?"

"Of course, of course," countered Flins, attempting to affix a more soothing tone to his speech. "It is just that I find it mildly surprising to find you here."

At that moment, Uliana appeared from her chamber, lovely eyes ablaze with cold anger.

"But then perhaps it is not so surprising at all."

The albino did not comment further on the matter, only excused himself by claiming there was another matter elsewhere for him to attend to. He and Skrzak left.

Flins turned to address Uliana.

"You and the boy are to be ready to leave within an hour's time. It should not be much of a burden on you, for there is virtually nothing you will be allowed to take with you." He glanced appreciatively at her body, her appealing curves. "Except, of course, the clothes you, ahem, wear on your back."

Then he reached out with a hand towards her face, extending two fingers to run along her cheek.

"I regret having to strike you before, Comrade. Perhaps there will be enough time yet for me to make my apologies?"

She snatched up his probing hand with her own, then began to bend the fingers back at inappropriate angles.

Uliana then heard the distinctive sound of the cocking of a pistol and felt cold steel caress her temple.

"No matter," said Flins, freeing his hand from her and pressing the gun into her head with the other. "I never cared much for reheated *borscht* anyway."

Uliana drifted silently backwards, away from the lieutenant and into her chamber. She flung its entrance covering back into place, removing her from Flins' sight.

The Russian lieutenant sighed, reholstered his pistol and then began the long walk back to the City.

The five engineers had continued to work around the clock, even in the absence of their master. To do so without interruption they had put their valleymen into a state of rest while they themselves increased their activity to bring about certain contingency plans of Dr. Evil himself.

Within their metal huts atop the giant platform, the engineers operated machines that had previously been brought to the caverns and painstakingly assembled there. The work was delicate, requiring exacting measures and precise control; a directive was being put in motion, one that would be brought to its final stages once the ultimate execution command was given.

No one of them was sure as to when that command would arrive, or how, but they had their orders.

They ran shifts, with one of them on lookout duty at all times. This engineer watched the surrounding chamber and its entrances for any sign of attack or other actions by the valleymen. After the capture of their master, the engineers found that, eventually, it seemed as if the dwellers of the subterranean world had left them to their own devices.

Then an alarm sounded within their prime control room. The engineer on watch duty signaled the others that someone was approaching their location.

It was to be expected. The engineers, capable of independent thought, knew that they would have to deal with the natives of the caverns eventually, but the hope was that they might finish their grand work before that moment arrived.

Surprisingly, a monitor screen showed just two figures standing alone in the audience chamber.

The watch-duty engineer zoomed in on the intruders, seeing that both of them wore the uniform of the Red Army; a lieutenant and a sergeant.

A speaker crackled to life within the machine filled room. A voice came through, speaking in Russian.

"We wish to talk," it said. "Things have changed."

XIX
SWAMP

They pushed him in and he tumbled end over end then slid down a steep decline. Trying to halt his slippery progress by repeatedly jamming one boot out to the side, he found the chute down which he fell to be too smooth to gain purchase.

His fellow prisoner had been put in before him, a minute or so before his own sentence was proclaimed once more, and then he too was plunged into the unknown. The moment they released his arms and he began to descend, he heard the rough scraping sound of heavy stone against stone behind him and knew with cold certainty that his entry point was no longer an escape option.

Reaching the bottom, he was flung out into open space and into total, complete darkness.

Captain Action stood up and looked around, eager to determine the nature of his prison, the Swamp.

The air was fetid, the stone beneath his feet damp; there were also small pools of water or some other liquid scattered about. He guessed the chamber he was in was fairly good-sized, judging by the way the sound carried and echoed around him.

He also had the uncomfortable feeling he was being watched.

Drake wasn't afraid of the dark, but he'd gotten a bit tired of the almost constant absence of real light in the world of the valleymen, sometimes wondering if he'd ever see the sun again.

For some reason that reminded him of his hat. It was no longer on his head.

The captain crouched and, with his hands, began feeling all about where he had landed. The wet stone felt clammy under his fingers and here and there he came into contact with what felt like moss or lichen. A strong, boozy aroma assailed his nostrils.

Finally, his fingertips brushed something unlike stone; thankfully, it was his hat.

He found the chute down which he fell to be too smooth to gain purchase.

Once it was back on his head, Captain Action flipped the miniature goggles down from the hat and rifled through the array of lenses. Then, with the cavern around him illuminated in a sickly glow, he set about getting to know his surroundings.

The area was huge, as he'd surmised. Roughly circular in overall shape, Drake could see that the chamber was fed by two large tunnels. Peering intently at the openings in the walls of the chamber, he found that the tunnels formed a kind of immense curve, intersecting the area in which he stood. Their walls were almost smooth, as if formed by the regular passage of something huge over a long period of time. Drake began to see the chamber as a kind of rest area just off a track or a road.

It also strangely reminded him of an underground larder.

That thought made him swing around in place, examining the floor of the chamber and its walls. He could see what, again, seemed like moss or some other parasitic growth crawling over the stone, ceiling, walls, and floor.

Then the captain spotted the opening of the chute down which he'd been pushed and Uliana's words came back to him: her people had once used the cavern for their waste disposal.

Captain Action then began to very seriously ponder the whereabouts of his fellow prisoner. Dr. Evil, a being no one in his right mind would trust, was nowhere to be seen.

A voice came at him from out of the darkness.

"How do you like my empire now, my friend?"

The captain wheeled around in a circle, looking through his lenses for his opponent. No one was there, or at least anywhere that he could see, though the voice couldn't be coming from very far away.

"Show yourself," he replied calmly.

The doctor's physiology was unlike any other human's, that he already knew, but Drake had never known the man to be literally cold-blooded. If true, he would fail to possess a heat signature for the captain to detect through his lenses.

"I don't think I will, captain. You seem too preoccupied with my position for me to feel secure. Let's just keep things as they are for now, eh?"

The captain tried a different tack. "I felt your unique presence several days ago, Dr. Tracy."

"That name no longer applies to me!" came the explosive response; a direct hit, thought Drake. The doctor had been known by the name Tracy before his mysterious transmutation into the despot called Dr. Evil. It was a sore point with the man, a goat easily gotten and one the A.C.T.I.O.N. agent had no compunction against exploiting.

Silence. Minutes later, the voice slithered out from the shadows once more, but fully in control of itself.

"Imagine, if you will, my dear captain, the great forest far above us on the surface. Imagine it is the year 1908.

"The Tunguska region is lit up like it is daytime, but it is only seven o'clock in the morning. Some say as if it were a second sun blazing overhead, come to visit the peoples of the area. Through the stress of its regard, no tree is left standing, no wildlife; just devastation."

Captain Action couldn't help but see it in his mind's eye, though it was somewhat difficult to picture, even harder to comprehend. To the scientists of the world, nothing like it had ever happened before in the annals of mankind. Perhaps only the dinosaurs had witnessed such a titanic blast in their kingdom of prehistory.

"This entire region, for miles all around us, was then bathed in a very special breed of radiation," said Dr. Evil. "It *seeped* into the world here, became one with the rocks, the stones, the very building blocks of the planet's crust, and below that, too. It metastasized with the Earth.

"I believe you already know of some of its properties, hmm? I shall not bore you with the litany then but only call out one of its most important traits: it eats energy. Sometimes ravenously so."

Drake pondered this as he began another circuit of the great cavern, searching every nook and cranny for his foe. The doctor's voice was filled with wonder, almost glee, and in the captain's experience that meant nothing good for anybody in his vicinity.

"I was meant to find it," said Evil with a note of triumph. "I was meant to conquer it."

"Following a trail of legends and tales and, yes, harder data, I made my way to this place after our, ahh, climactic meeting in China. And then, to my surprise and delight, I discovered an entire *city* below the earth; *directly below the affected area*!

"How easily controlled they are, these dwellers below. They have an innate, very natural will to protect and defend their home and their secret existence, a facet of their psyches that I simply tweaked a bit."

"Why?" spat out Captain Action.

"Why *what* exactly, my friend?"

"Why this takeover, why this radiation obsession, and why devote so many resources here?"

A low bit of laughter sounded in his ears, seemingly right next to him. Drake tamped down his surprise, figuring it for a trick of the acoustics.

"This city is not known to anyone else on Earth. Once I have conquered the secrets of the radiation, which I strongly believe to be extraterrestrial, I will use it to destroy the nuclear arsenals of the world, one by one, by sapping their radiation with my own. Then the countries will be eager to talk with me, and I shall, from my hidden base, oh, you know…

"…rule them all!"

Drake backed up from where he'd been standing until his spine touched the far stone wall, right next to one of the immense tunnel openings. From his vantage point, he believed he could see or sense anything that might suddenly come at him, from any angle.

"Not making much progress, are you?" he asked Evil with a sly smile in his voice. "You wanted to know before how I liked your 'empire.' Well, I can't say much for it, doctor. Seems to be mired in politics. And confusion."

The low sound of mirth again. "Oh, you believe your presence here has, what is it, thrown a monkey wrench into my plans? You think that because you survived my assassins I sent to the United States and made your way here that you have been a disruption?

"This city is *mine*, Captain. These people are *mine*. I am in complete command here."

"Then why," said Drake, "are you down here with me?"

No reply came back. Captain Action closed his eyes and opened his ears, straining them to capture every last scintilla of sound in the chamber. It was a trick he picked up while training for the SEALs, one that had served him well on other occasions.

He stilled his own breathing and listened very closely for a clue, any clue at all, to the location of Dr. Evil.

"I should like to use my new servants to my full advantage, outside these caverns," said the doctor finally, as if conducting a lecture in a classroom. "But, as you have witnessed, the radiation has become an integral, inseparable part of them over the years since 1908. Part of their very cells, their entire being.

"Here they live for many, many years. In the outside world they die. I must know why."

"Why are you here with me then?" Drake asked once more.

"Something keeps them alive in their city," continued Evil, as if he hadn't heard the captain's question. "Something that dulls the more destructive nature of the radiation. This element or substance or whatever it may be could also be used against me when I unleash the power of the radiation upon the nuclear missiles. That would be intolerable."

Captain Action was, he felt, getting his bearings. If only the man would continue jabbering away, he thought.

"Recently, I have come across a possible answer to the question. I have found someone who has lived outside this underground empire of mine and survived. For many years, in fact.

"Your woman, Captain. Your little buttercup; she is the key. She holds the answer."

That did it. The captain balled up his fist and swung his arm in a wide arc out to his immediate right, swiftly and with force.

It impacted something with a sickening thump.

As Drake guessed, Dr. Evil had been standing virtually right on top of him, just inside one of the tunnel entrances. Using the strange harmonics of the chamber, he'd thrown his voice and compounded the mystery of his whereabouts.

Captain Action heard his foe's cry of pain and flew at him like a spear. His fists shot out, landing sharp, jabbing blows on the doctor's jaw. Staggered and unable to defend himself, the madman went down hard and into a small puddle of moisture.

He lay there moaning until the captain, curious, strayed a bit too close and received a hammering kick to his leg for his folly. Evil was then suddenly and almost supernaturally up on his feet again and swinging at Drake, who stumbled backwards from a glancing thrust of his opponent's fist.

Separated and both breathing hard, each man waited for the other to make the next move.

"You idiot," said Drake, "don't you see? We can get out of here, both of us, if we do it *together*."

Evil barked like a hyena at that. "Who is the idiot, my old friend?" he inquired with a snort. "Don't *you* see?

"I *wanted* to be put in here! I subconsciously *ordered* that imbecile Bring to put me in here!"

Captain Action lunged at his foe, catching him off guard with a roundhouse kick. The doctor shuffled backwards, holding his stomach and breathing even harder. But still he laughed.

"Look-look around you...Captain," he wheezed. "Go ahead...I shall wait."

It wasn't a trick; that much Drake was sure of. There was most likely very little the doctor could trick him with in the chamber now that he had him in his sights.

"It's just another cave," he told his foe, taking a step towards him. "Now, are you going to work with me, or against me?"

"Please," implored Evil, putting up one hand for the captain to halt. "Another story, if you will."

Captain Action, against his better judgment, paused to listen.

"I have been here before," said the doctor, gesturing all round them. "A good emperor should know his kingdom inside and out. I had found a very, very old man in the city who had an incredible storehouse of knowledge in his brain. From it I learned of this place, almost forgotten by the city dwellers, but, to those who remembered, a place that was infused with its own legends."

"They threw their garbage away here," said Drake, shaking his head.

"Yes, yes, they did. That's very good, Captain. Very good. But do you know what happened to all that refuse, those waste materials? The answer lies behind you."

He glanced at the tunnels, loathe to look away from Evil for one single second. He noticed how slick the walls were, how much like an animal's warren it all seemed.

"I realized that *something* was down here, in these tunnels. And that it had awakened after a very long sleep, not long before I arrived.

"And it was hungry."

Drake covered the distance between him and his opponent in two steps and darted out with one hand to grab the doctor's collar. He looked down at the man's clothes; he wore a blue Nehru jacket that matched his iridescent pants and a golden medallion on a chain around his neck. The ensemble made him look like some twisted, nightmarish flower child.

Captain Action pulled the doctor closer and put on his best tough guy face.

"Get to the point," he growled. "What are you going on about?"

"It is coming," said Evil, smiling contemptuously in the darkness. "I can hear it. You should be able to hear it about now, too, even with those stunted, human ears of yours. And, hopefully, you will be able to comprehend it with that stunted, human brain of yours."

He let go of the man's collar and shoved him away. Evil sprawled awkwardly on the stone floor, but continued to smile and then titter underneath his breath.

Drake turned his back on him and faced one of the tunnels, standing at nearly the center point of the giant curve.

He felt a wind or some other kind of movement of the air. It suddenly occurred to him that it might be a displacement of the air coming down the tunnel.

Far off, he heard a faint scraping sound.

"Are you familiar with *Salamandrella keyserlingii*, Captain?"

Drake froze, said nothing. What he did was listen.

"Incredible species," said Dr. Evil. "Can exist in a state of, oh, let us call it hibernation, for *years* on end in the Siberian permafrost. Astounding. And that is just the small ones.

"What if the big ones could sleep for decades, perhaps even for a century?"

The captain was barely listening to the doctor. His every nerve was on edge, his entire being on alert. Somewhere, in the most primitive part of his brain, he felt a small tickle of fear. The fear of cold things. The fear of things that slither.

"Who is to say what it is now, even myself, in all my eminent wisdom, cannot be sure. But we have talked. I have introduced myself to it.

"I have extracted promises from it."

The scraping sound was louder now. It rustled down the tunnel like the sound of a hundred moles or a thousand rats. A raspy, labored breathing noise could also be heard. *Move*, he told himself. *Move!* he screamed inside his head.

Dr. Evil sat up, then crawled to his feet. He adjusted his clothing, flicked soil from his sleeves.

"Consider yourself privileged, Captain. You are about to meet my instrument of vengeance.

"King Zor is coming."

Captain Action looked over his shoulder at the doctor, tried to form a question, but failed and turned back to the tunnel.

Then he saw it.

XX
KING

It was a monstrous, abhorrent thing, an aberration of nature on a grand, matchless scale. Captain Action watched in shock as it extruded itself from the tunnel opening and into the cavern; he had to take several steps back to take it all in.

The body of it was at least thirty feet long, thick with blue-brown skin and purplish streaks. Hardened like armor from scraping along through tunnels of rock and stone, its leathery hide looked tough enough to withstand explosives. Drake also noticed a bony ridge down it lengthy spine and claws like giant spades on its stumpy fingers and toes.

The thing's tail was as long as its body and seemingly possessed a life all its own. It wound around, coiling and uncoiling, slapping against the surrounding rock. Even in his shock, the captain noticed an unhealed wound near the end of the tail, perhaps from a cave-in or a particularly sharp outcropping of rock.

He purposefully avoided looking at its eyes, but the lure of them was too much to ignore. Set high and on opposite sides of the gigantic head, the watery, alien orbs gave the surprising impression of intelligence. They revolved in its massive skull, taking in its surroundings, observing, classifying.

Drake's mind reeled at witnessing such a creature, but the scientific portion of his gray matter, the cold, reasoning half, tried to force the thing into neat little boxes. At that it failed. If the thing was related at all to the small salamanders of the region, as the doctor had suggested, it had risen far above such mundane origins. Grown to such a size, fed by the garbage of centuries? Mutated further by radiation?

It all had to be considered. Otherwise it was something out of legend, out of a Tolkien novel. And then it was far too unbelievable.

The thing was restless, that Captain Action could also see, but it did not advance farther, did not strike. Its eyes searched for meaning, much as his own did, but, for the moment, it seemed to be biding its time.

Dr. Evil stepped up beside him and the thing reared up, almost scraping the ceiling, and opened its monstrous jaws to release a sibilant, searing hiss.

"Is it not magnificent, Captain?"

Drake said nothing, unsure of mere words and their inability to frame his current thoughts. He fought the overwhelming urge to reach for his lightning sword, his electronic pistol; but, of course, they were not there.

"King Zor has come," said the doctor, wringing his blue hands. "An ancient name, lost to the recordings of history, but appropriate for a beast of its stature, its elegant bearing."

Evil glanced over at his foe, smiling at the captain's stillness.

"Ah, yes, the natural human loathing of reptiles, magnified a thousandfold. A pity that you cannot appreciate King Zor as I do. But you always were a dullard, unable to grasp what my more advanced brain easily seizes upon."

"You say you *know* this thing?" stammered Captain Action. He took several more steps backwards. Zor grumbled low in its throat, watching him with its calculating eyes.

The doctor shook his head, almost a ludicrous sight when involving a man with an exposed brain.

"Captain, haven't you been listening? Please note the small modification I have made there."

He pointed to the creature's head. Drake followed the line from his pointing finger and was surprised to see a small metal device attached to the thing's skull, just above its neck, but below its eye line. It blinked on and off, signifying some activity. He turned and looked at Evil.

"You're insane. If I didn't fully know it before, I know it now."

"What you see is not *insanity*, my friend," said the doctor. "What you see is my 'ticket to ride,' as the young ones among your kind would say.

"King Zor is my chariot, my vehicle back to the City above us. There I shall address a few, ahh, pressing issues and know this, Captain: if I cannot have my empire, no one shall. That is a promise."

Captain Action watched in horror as his opponent reached up and dug his thin blue fingers down in between his grotesque, mottled brain and the half-skull that cradled it like a coddled egg.

The young man tore at the massive stone covering. Sweat beaded on his forehead as he tried desperately to move the carved and shaped rock away from the chute to the Swamp and free his mentor.

Sean looked up to see Uliana enter the chamber. His eyes were that of the possessed, wild and pitiable.

"Help me!" he cried out to the woman. "C'mon! We can move this thing together! Just-just...help me..."

He strained at the stone, pulling at its sides; Uliana could see that his fingers were bloody from his useless exertions. She ran up to him, grabbed him by the shoulders.

"Sean! Sean, listen to me!" she implored the young man. "This is not what you want to be expending your energy on, trust me."

He looked up at her as one who finds a traitor in his midst. Uliana ignored the look and enfolded Sean in her arms.

"It is hard to hear," she whispered to him, "but it is true. You cannot move the stone away from the entrance to the Swamp. It is the work of many men, not one brave, fearless young man who wants to help his friend."

She pulled back, still holding Sean by the arms, but squaring her face with his.

"Sean, he is dead to us. Yes, yes, I know but we must make our own way now.

"War is coming."

Uliana then looked over Sean's shoulder to see Bury enter the chamber, sad-eyed and wagging his head.

"I'm not sure what you are telling the boy," he said to her in their language, "but I sense it is important. Perhaps you should also tell him that we need to leave this area and return to a safer place."

The woman's anger flared and she stepped away from Sean to approach her father's brother.

"That I have to slink around my own people, my own home and...and..."

Bury held up his hands in a gesture of surrender.

"You are the First Brighten. You are my brother's daughter. I watched as you were cast out all those turn-cycles ago and said nothing. I thought you would be a thing of wonder to our City when you were born, but instead you were scorned and, perhaps, feared. It wasn't fair, but you were strange to many, and people fear what is strange to them."

"I'm not ashamed of who I am! Not anymore!"

"And well you should not be," he placated her. "What you should be ashamed of, as I am, is the knot of sickness that exists within our kinsmen's hearts. I cannot understand it. I never would have guessed that such evil could grow here. Bring was always ambitious. It was he who first organized the Free against this blue-skinned villain. But now, his alliance with these…these…*Russians*?"

Bury's eyes traveled from the brown orbs of Uliana to the clearing eyes of Sean Barrett. The young man had found his center, he could see, and was stifling his pain for the tasks ahead.

"Let us leave this place," he told them both, tired and shaken. "As you say, war is coming and we should be among allies."

A meeting of the City tribunal had been called. Its members sequestered themselves in their room in their high tower and got down to the business of planning a war.

Language had continued to be a problem between the Soviets and their valleymen counterparts, but they were advancing on it and finding ways to communicate. What both sides were finding in common was a mirrored thirst for power.

There also existed among the assembled a desire to come out on top when the current situation was finally settled. This desire festered in the hearts of both the soldiers and the dwellers below, unbeknownst to each other.

"We agree then," proclaimed Flins, "that we rule together. For our mutual benefit."

In his own mind, the Russian lieutenant had absolutely no intention of sharing anything, much less rulership over the underground world.

He'd promised the valleymen to supply them with arms and other equipment once the malcontents among them were rooted out and dealt with. Playing up the great benefits of Russian technology and the wider world that would be opened to the dwellers, he cajoled the subhumans to throw in with him and together bring the City under their joint control.

The control of the Union of Soviet Socialist Republics, he told himself coldly. Flins would be decorated and feted and promoted once he exposed this incredible valley of resources to the party; he would have everything he ever dreamed of, finally.

Though the lieutenant had come to despise his colonel general, Veles had taught him one thing: do unto others as you would have them do unto you. In other words, the world was full of backstabbers. Stab them first before they could pull their own knives on you.

Focusing on the present, he looked at the man across the table from him and wondered for a moment if it was indeed the one they called by the ridiculous name "Bring." Flins was honestly not sure; they all looked alike to him, these dirty, ragged City people.

"…are happy to lock hands with you," Bring was saying. "Too long have our kinsmen sat and wallowed here Below and ignored the treasures of Above. Now we can finally be rid of those among us who stand in the way of advancement."

Flins listened closely, then conferred with one of his soldiers who felt he understood the valleymen's language a little better than others.

"Yes," said the lieutenant, nodding in an overstated, patronizing fashion, "we can now make a plan to wipe out the rest of our enemies. It shouldn't take too long, seeing as there are so few of them left."

Someone cleared his throat at the far end of the table. Flins rolled his eyes covertly and glanced down at his fellow lieutenant, Marowit.

The man was in bad shape. Wounded from a fight with a valleyman under the thrall of Dr. Evil, his condition worsened by the minute. There were no adequate facilities in the City to address his wounds and they pained the man greatly.

He looked like death warmed over, thought the god of death.

"Yes, Comrade?" he asked Marowit.

"We cannot, as I have told you before," said the ashen-faced, gaunt lieutenant, "underestimate Juthrbog's involvement with these people and with that woman, Comrade."

"Yes, but, *Comrade*," replied Flins patiently, "I have told *you* that once we have removed the woman from the scene, he will fall in line. He is a man of duty, as we are, comrade. He is not too far gone yet."

Marowit coughed, a fine spray of blood issuing from between his lips. "But, *Comrade*, there are no guarantees of that! That white-skinned freak will be our undoing! He must be dealt with *now*!"

The lieutenant pounded the table weakly, bending over it and looking up at Flins through rheumy eyes encircled in grey.

"No," said Flins resignedly, "I'm afraid it is *you* that must be dealt with now, Comrade."

And so he took out a pistol and planted a bullet between his fellow lieutenant's eyes. The sudden hole leaked crimson and Marowit closed his eyes and quietly put his head down.

Flins looked back at the abruptly apprehensive faces of the valleymen.

"Simply burying what was already dead, my friends. Now may we proceed with our plans?"

From some place between the bowl of his skull and his hideous brain, Dr. Evil removed a small metal capsule. He held it between his fingers, turning it this way and that.

"The key, dear Captain," he said with a note of satisfaction.

Peering through his lenses, Drake saw the little capsule suddenly pop open in the doctor's hand. Its shell then fell away, revealing a tiny apparatus that resembled a minute magnifying glass.

Evil depressed a tiny stud on the device, its handle telescoped, and the disc at its top somehow expanded in size. When the actions ceased, the instrument was at least double its size and now fit more comfortably in its owner's hand.

Dr. Evil raised one eyebrow in devilish fashion and brought the disc of the device near to his mouth. His lips parted and he spoke into it.

"King Zor – *come here!*"

The Monster reared back suddenly and hissed.

Captain Action, having once again found his steely composure, leapt out of the way as the thing's immense tail whipped forward and slammed down where he formerly stood. The floor of the cavern erupted in a spray of stone chips, dust, and moisture.

Dr. Evil jumped back, too, a strange expression on his twisted features. The captain realized his foe was confused.

"Zor!" the doctor spat into his device. "Obey! Stand back! Stand back, I tell you!"

Drake ran several yards to one side, eyeing the creature and estimating its trajectory.

"I think your friend here doesn't care for your 'modification,' doctor," he called out. "Don't you know it's not nice to fool with Mother Nature?"

Evil wheeled around, fury etched into his face. "I cannot comprehend it! I was in control of it before!"

Captain Action darted swiftly and neatly towards his foe and slammed into him as if he were taking down a quarterback.

In their wake, a gigantic paw sporting gleaming claws swiped through the air, narrowly missing them both.

The captain grabbed for the doctor's control device. He found it to be locked in the iron grip of his fellow prisoner.

"Imbecile!" cried Evil, scrambling away from him. "You should hope, *pray* that I again gain command over Zor; the alternative will not be to your liking!"

As if in response, the thing reared up once more, this time impacting with the high ceiling of the cavern. The resulting explosion of stone and sound deafened Captain Action and sent him sprawling away from the creature and the rain of debris.

Recovering from the roll he'd executed to gain as much distance from Zor as possible, he stood, turned, and looked.

The creature had gone completely berserk.

Dr. Evil was also gone. Or, at least, Drake could no longer make him out in the darkness.

He peered up at the opening to the chute down which he and the doctor had originally tumbled. Too high up the cavern wall for him to reach, he quickly abandoned that option.

"A minor setback," came a voice in his ear.

The captain jerked around to find his foe standing right next to him. Before he himself even knew what was happening, the man's throat was between his hands and he was applying pressure.

Behind them, the monster thrashed and hissed, shaking the very structure of the chamber.

"*Now* do you want to work together, Doctor?" Drake asked through gritted teeth. "I think you'd better make a decision fast."

"I controlled it before," Evil whispered meekly. "Cannot understand it."

Suddenly, with the sounds of the creature ringing in Drake's ears, and his most hated foe's throat between his fingers, clarity of thought arrived.

Captain Action understood it.

XXI
CONTROL

Slippery like an eel, Dr. Evil broke free from the captain and pitched headlong towards King Zor. In his outstretched hand he held the small controller.

Drake watched spellbound as the doctor placed one hand on his temple and moved the controller close to his blue lips. Then a look of intense concentration spread over his face, and Drake could have sworn the man's brain pulsed and expanded in its skull socket.

"Zor," intoned Dr. Evil, "you will obey. You...will...*obey*."

The towering lizard thrashed less, then lowered its head and oriented itself towards the commands. Its enormous tail continued to whip back and forth, knocking loose stones from the wall of the cavern as it appeared to listen intently to the doctor's words.

Captain Action noticed that the creature was even less like a salamander than he first thought; it appeared more like a dinosaur, in fact, especially concerning its rear legs in proportions to its arms. Again he marveled at the forces that created such a monster. If he wasn't stuck far underground in an increasingly small chamber with it, he might have called it the marvel of the 20th century.

But as it was, he could only see it as a force of destruction and a potential tool of Dr. Evil.

Stepping towards it, slowly, the doctor continued his intonations and concentration. Zor's head drifted back and forth on its neck, waving through the air in a dreamy manner. Then a ripple ran down from its neck and across its entire body. Drake wondered if the thing were trying to resist Evil's commands, its body attempting to reject whatever hold the villain might have over it.

Regardless, he was going to have to act, and act soon.

Dr. Evil stopped his mantra abruptly and turned to Captain Action.

"There, you see; as docile as a kitten and fully in my power."

"I find that hard to believe," remarked Drake, pointing a thumb at Zor.

"This kind of stuff usually finds a way of biting you in the butt."

The doctor's face lost its sheen of enjoyment. He frowned.

"Not this time," he grumbled. "This time, the bite is on you." He brought the controller to his mouth once again and directed an index finger at the captain.

"Zor, fetch."

Captain Action leaned down and, in one smooth movement, scooped up a jagged shard of stone and hurled it at Zor.

The pointed barb of rock smashed against the creature's tail, hitting the fresh wound Drake had seen earlier.

Zor screamed, rearing up on its legs, its eyes nearly popping out of its head searching for its torturer.

The captain ran as Dr. Evil bellowed behind him.

He ran towards the tunnels.

The thing's tail whipped about furiously, cracking rock and smashing stone. Drake was swiftly closing in on the closest tunnel's entrance when the massive log of a tail was suddenly in his path, hurtling directly at him.

He dove like a swimmer, like a thrown jackknife. The tail missed him by inches.

He came down in a rolling somersault and landed deftly on his feet. Spotting another likely missile, he shot another barb at the creature's wound.

With the resulting screech from Zor echoing through the cavern, Captain Action quickly sprinted down the tunnel and was soon enveloped in darkness.

That should put a bee in its bonnet, he thought to himself. Dr. Evil's control should be slipping just about now.

King Zor chased after the little man. Its tail burned with pain and the thing in its head answered that pain with a sting of its own.

Down the tunnel it slithered, feeling better in its cool embrace. It felt that the pain in its head lessened the farther into the shadows it moved. With its giant nostrils sucking greedily at the air, it hoped it would find its attacker soon. And that it might taste good.

It had been so very, very long since it'd had anything good to eat.

Up ahead the tunnel sloped upwards and widened, eventually opening up somewhat into a resting place, an even cooler spot. Zor raced towards it.

There was some kind of noise behind its tail, though, a small squeak of a voice. It told Zor what to do, what to do with the little man when he was

Zor screamed, rearing up on its legs... The captain ran as Dr. Evil bellowed behind him.

found. He didn't like the voice.

Then he came to a stop in the resting spot.

There was the man, standing right in front of Zor.

But it wasn't the man. It was someone else, someone else the creature knew.

It was one of the biggest gambles he'd ever bet on. Forget disguising himself as the general secretary of the entire USSR; this was even more daunting.

Captain Action stepped out into the path of Zor and held up a hand for it to stop.

On his face he wore the scholarly, almost kindly countenance of Dr. Ling.

Drake called to mind the voice Evil used when disguised as Ling and then projected that voice out into the tunnel. It was a one-in-a-million roll of the dice, but there'd be no escaping the monstrous thing otherwise. The odds were poor no matter how they were figured.

He had retained the Ling mask after he'd torn it off his foe's face up on the balcony, so long ago it seemed. His intention was to keep it as a last resort, to use it if he needed to become Ling to allow them to leave the underground world. Now he was wearing it to stop a monster.

Its material was no plastidrem, but the mask was mostly intact and fit almost like a second skin. Combined with the captain's acting abilities, it provided him with the edge he needed to potentially beat the doctor at his own game.

King Zor slowed, then stopped. It looked at Drake. It snorted once, then twice. He could feel the thing's hot, acrid breath on his face, even through the mask.

He thought, though, that it might be working.

The lizard hesitated, then laid its gigantic body down flat across the floor of the tunnel. Its eyes never left the man who stood in front of it as it moved into what he guessed to be a comfortable position.

Drake began to talk, low at first, but then louder.

"Zor, it is I, Zor. I have found you at last. We have met before, do you remember? Yes, that's right. I am your friend."

"What are you doing?" came a loud, explosive voice. Dr. Evil ran up and around Zor, directly at Captain Action. The doctor's hands curled into claws as he grasped at the Ling face.

The captain floored him with one punch, then quickly swung his attention back to the beast. Zor snorted again, raised its head slightly, but, seeing what had just transpired, lowered it back again.

Drake leaned down and picked up the controller that Evil had dropped. He spoke into it; platitudes at first, then just words he felt might be soothing to the thing. The combination of the Ling face and the device exerted a fine control over Zor, or so it seemed.

Now he just had to figure out exactly what to do with the creature.

For their first declaration of war, the tribunal shut off traffic between the City of New Lake and the Outer Chambers and the Gardens. The dwellers therein protested, but were ignored.

Valleymen and Russian soldiers were then posted in the connecting tunnels between the two areas, all armed.

Shortly before the action, Flins had discovered that some of his men were gone from their temporary barracks in the City, Juthrbog and Skrzak among them. The lieutenant cursed to himself over the act of defiance, then to everyone around him.

Holding back his temper even further when he found that the cache of weapons they'd discovered after ousting Dr. Evil had been pilfered, Flins moved his timetable ahead and gave orders for the first sortie to commence.

So be it, he said aloud. He had everything and everyone he needed to mount his campaign; the City would be his soon, he thought, and when it was there'd be some new rules in place.

His rules.

The gardens erupted with gunfire. At a nod from a lightning sword-wielding Uliana, Juthrbog gave the order for his men to return fire. Soon the very rock of the valleymen's once private, untainted kingdom was forever soiled by spilled blood.

The Russian lieutenant had returned with the little company clerk to report that his attempt to negotiate with Dr. Evil's engineers had borne no fruit; the mysterious lackeys of the former tyrant had refused to talk, and Juthrbog was certain they were up to no good. They were working on something, he told Uliana; some directive perhaps from Evil himself before he went down the chute.

The albino's entire demeanor changed when he talked to her, she noticed. The only comfort she found in it was that he was most likely not lying to her about the engineers.

Sean Barrett insisted on a gun for himself. Uliana had thought it over and decided it was for the best, for the young man to protect himself. He also had his protective garments, which he insisted on referring to as made from "space-age materials." Whether or not the gear could stop a bullet, well, she tried not to think about it.

For herself, Uliana carried Captain Action's sword and a pistol, figuring she was a product of both worlds, one Above and one Below. All those around her were drawn to the sight of the sword in her hand.

Her own thoughts were not so ordered, unfortunately. They tended to stray to Miles Drake, to their short time together. Regretfully she shoved them to the side and centered on what she had to do to save her home.

If Captain Action were still alive, somewhere, she told herself that he'd do the same thing. The thought comforted her as she stepped forward to clear New Lake of invaders once and for all.

Uliana had dreamed many times throughout her life in Russia about what her homecoming might be like. Though she was certain that there might be some lingering hostility awaiting her, never once had she imagined it quite like the war that erupted all around her now.

Captain Action toed the prostrate form of Dr. Evil, one eye still on King Zor. The creature seemed content for the moment to lay there and simply look in his direction.

"Get up," he said. "I know you're awake."

The man stirred, then sat up, glowering.

"I'm going to need you to be quiet. Our giant monarch here doesn't seem to care much for the sound of your voice. Can't say I blame him much."

"You will never be able to remain in complete control of it," said Evil, matter-of-factly. "No matter what subterfuge you use. Zor is more intelligent than you realize."

"So far," remarked Drake, "my 'subterfuge' is paying off. I figured you must have appeared as Ling, gentler than your usual big, bad evil self, when you approached this thing previously. Especially since you had to get close enough to implant that device."

He pointed to the blinking control box on the lizard's head, then brought the controller up to his lips.

"Zor, listen to me."

The massive beast stirred. It opened its mouth slightly, and a kind of hum issued forth.

"I need to go somewhere. Somewhere up above." Drake pointed upwards, over his head. Zor followed his hand, gazing up at the craggy ceiling of the rest spot.

"Will you help?" he asked it. "*Can* you help?" he said more to himself than anything.

The creature's mighty tailed flicked back and forth. Captain Action could see that it was favoring the wound there, keeping it turned inward, away from him and Dr. Evil.

Finally, King Zor raised itself up on its haunches and nosed around the ceiling, sniffing at it. It jabbed then at it a few times, producing a small shower of stones.

"Well," said the captain, "I think maybe we have our way out of here. Doctor, I thank you most sincerely for the idea and the loan of, ahh, 'Ling' here.

"Why don't we just step out of the way now? If I've guessed correctly and we're in roughly the best spot for what I have in mind, I believe a few people up there are in for a big surprise"

He began to walk farther down the tunnel, making sure that the beast could see him, see that kindly old Dr. Ling wasn't abandoning him.

Dr. Evil stood up, dusted himself off and looked up at his foe.

"Wait for me. I can still be of some use. You will see."

XXII
BREAKOUT

King Zor began to move stone and dirt. It dug its armored snout into the walls and ceiling of the tunnel, breaking loose great sheets of their substance and then scrabbling to push it away with its small, clawed fingers.

"It is an incredible machine," remarked Dr. Evil of the sight. He and Captain Action stood far back from the mound of debris that was quickly piling up around the beast. The captain was also standing away from the doctor, still wary of tricks from his opponent.

Miles Drake felt a wave of heightened awareness flow through him as he monitored Zor's progress. Deep inside him he sensed an urgent panic that flooded through the entire area; something was transpiring above them, in the City and its environs. Something that made his yearning to break free of his prison even more intense.

"Where are you directing it?" his fellow prisoner inquired. "King Zor is not a force of nature to be pointed willy-nilly out into the wider world. It is a force of nature to be used with *purpose*, with precision."

"You'll see." Evil's commentary was beginning to annoy him. He longed to get back to the City level, though Drake knew he'd still have to ultimately deal with Dr. Evil, one way or another. It would be a long haul back to civilization with him in tow.

The doctor moved closer to the captain.

"Here; you are woefully underutilizing the beast. If you would simply consider my suggestions. I, of course, am the one with the intimate knowledge of Zor's capabilities."

Captain Action threw out one arm to hold him off, never taking his eyes and the face of Ling from the gigantic powerhouse of an animal.

"No! Plant yourself, Doctor; I don't want to have to tell you again!"

"And *I*," said Evil menacingly, "do not want to have to see you live any further."

Reaching once again between his exposed brain and his skull, he pulled something out with a wet slurping sound and then leapt at Drake. Going in low, the doctor stabbed at his foe's back, just above his belt. Making contact, he pushed and twisted his hand.

The captain felt a sharp pain, then a warmth. Reflexively he knocked Dr. Evil back with a single blow, then felt around at the stinging area on his back.

There he found a short, collapsible blade sticking out of him.

He knew the controller was being taken from his fingers. He knew it, but could seem to do nothing about it. Perhaps there was some variety of drug on the blade.

Dr. Evil danced away from him and closer to King Zor. Drake watched as the man held the device up to his mouth and spoke into it.

Reaching to his lower back again, the captain bit down on his tongue and pulled the knife out with a single tug. It felt as if he'd uncorked a bottle and allowed the contents to gush forth.

A hideous sound from the giant lizard swung him back around to face it dizzily.

Zor had stopped its digging. The air of the tunnel was choked with dust from the activity, making it hard for Drake to breathe. He held one hand over the wound, trying to stop the bleeding. It wasn't doing much good.

"Obey!" shouted Dr. Evil. "Obey me! We will be leaving this place and moving along to another location! Listen to me!"

The monster crouched down from the excavation sight, trying to see his master. Evil swiftly turned his back on it, hoping to hide his bluish countenance from the thing's probing vision.

Captain Action fell to his knees, the pain searing him with its intensity. He tried to fight it off, tried to call up techniques he'd learned all over the globe for working through such a monumental injury.

"You are beaten, Captain!" yelled Dr. Evil, triumphantly. "This is my empire! It is me and I am it! Forever!"

King Zor saw the fallen Ling, felt the burning sensation in its head. It also saw the other man, the one who'd caused it pain before.

It reared up and roared.

Drake saw and felt throughout every fiber of his being an entire wall of the tunnel cave in. The amount of rock that sloughed off and came crashing down into the area was overwhelming. It fell in huge chunks, the sound of its impact deafening.

And in the middle of it stood Dr. Evil, still screaming, still ranting, still waving his arms in victory.

The emperor of the subterranean world was soon buried in it.

He was unsure of exactly how much time had passed when he returned to consciousness. Covered in dirt and dust and rock and stone, he lay there for several minutes, attempting to take inventory of his body and his mind.

Finally, slowly, he tried to move. Everything screamed at him; his arms, his legs, and, with a special cry of despair, his back. But he forced himself to move everything so everything could prove to him that it still worked.

A rumbling sound came to his dirt-choked ears. He thought it might be thunder, a storm off in the distance, but, after a moment, he remembered where he was and discounted his first impression of the sound.

Turning his head, he saw only inky darkness. Then his fingers found his hat only inches from his head and he felt around for its goggles. Placing the hat on his head, he wiped away at the lenses to find, to his chagrin, one of them smashed beyond repair. Still, with the other lens active, he had a rudimentary idea of what was going on around him.

King Zor was digging again, all on its own.

Captain Action climbed up a pile of rock, wincing at the pain in his back. He'd managed to tear the sleeve off his uniform and fashion a bandage of sorts for his wound. Knowing full well that any jolt or extreme movement could reopen the wound, he gingerly made his way up the jumble of debris.

In front of him waved the tail of the monster.

Zor continued to dig, to burrow a new tunnel up to the chambers above. It did so at an angle that pleased Drake, allowing him to climb in its wake. Every so often, though, he had to move to avoid a small avalanche of stone and soil and his wound sang out again.

Then a great hissing from above him and a mighty rush of air told the captain that the beast had broken through.

He steeled himself for what would come next.

He pulled himself up into the open air of a large area. Light assaulted his eyes; though dim, it lanced through him. He blinked and then flipped the broken goggles back up into his cap.

Captain Action saw that he had estimated right: King Zor had brought them out into the audience chamber.

Zor's exit hole was on the far side of the cavern, a fair distance from the metal platform. The beast skulked around the area, suspicious of what it had found at the end of its digging. It sensed that Drake had also appeared there and turned to look at its master. It was then that the captain realized he still wore the mask of Dr. Ling.

The sound of metal clanging against metal rang through the chamber. He looked over to see the doors of some of the huts on the platform spring open and Dr. Evil's engineers step out.

Beneath his mask he smiled grimly.

He then began to trot towards the lizard, pointing at the platform. Without the controller, he wasn't sure what kind of direction Zor would take, but he intended to do everything in his power to get his idea through the thick skull of the world's largest cold-blooded monster.

"Zor!" he shouted, waving his arms at the huts. "Enemies! Attack! Attack! Go get 'em, boy!"

The Engineers pushed their frozen-with-fear valleymen out of their way and opened fire on the thing. The dwellers jumped off the platform and to the ground below.

Great gouts of gunfire lashed out at Zor. Five engineers pumped tremendous amounts of lead at the creature, peppering its skin from head to tail. The lizard thrashed about, rearing up and down, its tail cracking back and forth like a whip.

Drake wondered at first if bullets could hurt the thing, but after the initial rounds failed against its toughened skin, the engineers switched to armor-piercing slugs. The next hail of gunplay tore into the lizard, sending up sprays of thick, dark blood.

King Zor, insane with fury, charged the platform.

The skull-helmeted men held their ground, firing away as the immense creature plunged towards them like a freight train. Captain Action braced himself for the impact.

Suddenly King Zor's head exploded in a detonation of bone and flesh. Drake saw a flash of what looked like a small bazooka from the platform, then the headless body of the monster was crashing into the metal framework with a sickening, bone-jarring explosion of sound and destruction.

The platform collapsed. The metal huts caved in on themselves and went down with the entire structure in an orgy of bending girders and popping rivets.

Once the sounds died down, Captain Action saluted the great beast and then ran towards the scene of its sacrifice.

Ripping off the mask of Ling, he hurled it to the ground and approached the fiery blaze that resulted from the crash. The smell of the cooking flesh of Zor was monstrous and he staggered under its aroma. Then, catching sight of movement in the wreckage, the captain crouched low to try to see around and below the smoke.

The arm of an engineer stuck up out from between two twisted, smoking girders. Its sleeve was in ribbons but the glove mostly intact. Drake then spotted the helmet of the man and realized it had probably saved the engineer's skull from being crushed in the collapse.

The hand reached up to a bank of machinery, which appeared to be relatively intact, despite the horrendous damage to the huts and the platform. The fingers closed and opened, closed and opened, searching for something. Captain Action saw too late the object of the engineer's quest: a lever.

Before he could wade in and reach it, the man grasped the lever and pulled it down.

Nothing happened. Captain Action had tensed for it, anticipating a blast or something equal parts diabolical and explosive, but nothing seemed to come from the lever being thrown.

The engineer's hand then released the lever and slumped, lifeless.

Drake stood there, contemplating what he'd witnessed. He regretted the loss of life and, strangely enough, most especially that of King Zor.

His back ached. Everything ached, but he was alive and that was always preferable to the alternative.

He heard yelling and screaming then and turned to see a small group of people running towards him. In the lead was Sean Barrett. Suddenly alarmed, Drake threw up his hands to try and hold the young man off.

It was useless. Sean zoomed up and grabbed his mentor in a bear hug, whooping and shouting in his ear. He almost collapsed from the fresh pain in his back.

The young man must have realized something was wrong, for he pulled back and looked at the captain with an expression of concern and confusion.

Then the rest of the crowd of people were on him and he took them all in: Bury, Sing, other valleymen, Juthrbog and Skrzak, and Uliana.

She stared at him, hands at her sides but fingers clutching and unclutching. Tears welled up around the corners of her eyes as she mumbled something under her breath. Drake thought perhaps it was a curse of some kind.

He nodded at her, dizzy and confused. Turning his back to her he lifted up his uniform shirt.

"How does that look?" he asked, pointing at his wound. "It's pretty bad, isn't it?"

Uliana reached out and gently probed the surrounding area with her long fingers. He closed his eyes, wincing as she examined him.

"Not bad," she said, crying, smiling. "It looks like it cut through muscle at an angle. I have seen worse."

"Good, good," he said, his legs finally buckling.

After he was moved back to chambers far away from the destruction and from the Russian's first volley in the war, Captain Action lay on his side while the lovely Uliana cleaned and dressed his injury.

"And that's what's been happening," Sean finished. "We're at war. Any moment now we're gonna be overrun by Ruskies."

He looked suddenly up at Juthrbog. "Err, no offense, ahh, Comrade."

If the soldier understood him, he gave no evidence of such.

"What does it mean," asked Uliana, checking her work, "the pulling of the lever?"

Drake pondered that as he swung his feet back to the floor and sat up.

"Let's hope it means nothing. We have a lot more on our hands to worry about now."

In secret locations around the City and around the caverns that surrounded it, shutters swung open on large metal boxes.

These boxes came in pairs, their shuttered sides facing each other. They were placed in areas were they could not be seen.

From inside one of the boxes of each pair, out from between their shutters, a glow now emanated.

XXIII

HOSTILITIES

They marched down the long darkened corridor that led to the City, Captain Action and Uliana on point. Juthrbog walked one step behind and to one side, with Bury on his other side and a rank and file of Russian soldiers and valleymen following.

It had to be the strangest military assemblage Drake had ever witnessed.

Sean Barrett, though, was absent; the captain had ordered the boy to stay behind. This was made very clear to him. There'd be no rebellion on his part this time.

Bury and Uliana had told Drake that the large passageway was the only way in or out of the City, so far as they knew. They all agreed that a second sortie from their enemies would be one more too many, that they would be taking the high road and try to clean out the rats' nest in a more direct manner.

The small, cobbled-together army encountered resistance almost immediately.

With lightning sword in his hand, Uliana had gratefully relinquished it, Captain Action strode up to the blockade and announced himself. He wagered the soldiers to be too intelligent to fire on him in cold blood and the valleymen too uncertain to attack.

For his hubris, he received the news of his mistake with much sound and fury.

"I feel as if they will not be very receptive to parlaying," said Uliana sweetly as she drew back under fire.

"Beginning to think you may be right," answered Drake, trying to get an idea of what they were up against while ducking at the same time.

"It's the only access to our homes," noted Bury, "as I told you. If you can engage these men, I can get past them and into the City."

"And then what?" the captain queried.

"I shall try to convince my kinsmen to oust the Russians. This is all too much; it must end. If you can handle *your* people, I can deal with *mine.*"

Uliana returned Drake's troubled gaze. "If anyone can do this thing, *he* can, Captain." Gunfire suddenly splattered on the rocks nearby and she flinched. "And I agree this has gone on far too long."

Captain Action sighed, but did so without sounding defeated.

"Go," he told the valleyman. "We'll hold them here."

The soldiers engaged their own fellows, while the dwellers below moved in to confront their own kinsmen. The sound of battle rang throughout the caverns. Each squeeze of a trigger brought a deafening reverberation that ate away at the very souls of those who fought.

Juthrbog moved against his own men, those who chose to follow Flins into his valley of death rather than abandon the underground world to its owners. The lieutenant closed off that part of his mind that told him he was raising arms against those he once led; for those few, violent moments, he was simply a machine.

Captain Action rushed in with the valleymen, opting for hand-to-hand combat rather than toting a firearm. It was no less deadly, though, no less foolhardy, to lead the subterranean people against their own, than to pick off Red Army regulars with a borrowed firearm.

It was arduous fighting; cloaked in darkness and in strange surroundings, he lost his bearing more times than he cared to count. Only the steady sound of Uliana breathing next to him provided any grounding.

In the middle of the skirmish, he saw Bury slink along the side of the tunnel and then disappear.

Drake prayed the man had gotten through and to the other side.

Then, after a sense of time had left him, their opponents pulled back in retreat. It was as if someone had abruptly pulled the plug from a sink filled with water.

Captain Action called out for his men not to pursue but to hold their positions and secure the crossing. Within minutes the A.C.T.I.ON. agent was certain that they'd won the round and that the artery between the City and the Outer Chambers was theirs.

Uliana looked around at the dead and the wounded, shaking her head.

"Why does this not feel like a victory?" she asked him, her voice thin and tired.

"Because it's not; victory will come when we walk out of this place, every one of us who doesn't belong here."

Their eyes met and for a second the unanswered question of their future came into view. Then, in unspoken unison, they both turned back to the task at hand.

Corralling and reorganizing the soldiers and valleymen, the captain led them down the tunnel and into the City proper.

The City Chamber seemed much the same as it had on previous occasions, save for an unnameable quiet that hung over it, not unlike the ever-present mist. Drake scanned the buildings, unsure of what to look for or what to expect. He assumed it, whatever "it" would be, would come sooner than later.

Suddenly the ground before him erupted. A valleyman, perhaps eager to be in the presence of the wonders of New Lake once more, had moved forward and into the line of fire. He was cut to ribbons by submachine gun fire.

Captain Action bellowed out orders for everyone to move back. With the deafening roar of bullets crashing all around them, the little regiment retreated into the opening of the access tunnel and found cover there.

Uliana and Juthrbog appeared at his side, hunkering down with him.

"There, there, and there," the lieutenant pointed. "You see these emplacements, *da*? How very typical of my fellow Cossacks."

Uliana glowered, pounding one fist on the rocks of the tunnel wall.

"They are using the building as a fort! It was once the place where the produce from the Gardens was brought, where we would begin to work with it, and…"

She had lost her words. Drake resisted the urge to comfort her.

Before them was a structure which sat at the outermost corner of the City, a tall, multileveled building made of interconnecting stones. To the captain's mind it looked almost medieval in its construction, if, in fact, the people of a thousand years prior had developed the skills to construct towering, freestanding structures. In all it was a beautiful piece of otherworldly architecture, but it was now also malevolent, subverted for the use of death instead of life.

He understood and sympathized with the woman's anguish over the evil which had befallen her long-ago home.

"We've got to get past this," he told them. "Won't be easy, I know, but this is only the early stages of our mission. If we don't move past this, we might as well turn around and head back to the Outer Chambers."

"Then, what do you propose, Comrade?" asked the albino, a hint of weariness threading through his voice.

Drake's steely eyes ran over the problem, tried to look at it from every angle. It wasn't just tactics, wasn't just strategy. A straightforward military solution wasn't always the best answer.

"I'm going in," he said finally.

The Russian audibly scoffed at that, told the captain exactly what he thought of that plan.

"You might as well wear a target on your tunic," he said, scanning Drake's action uniform. "Will you also wave your magic sword as you advance?"

Captain Action ignored the man, focused on Uliana.

"Help me."

"How?" she asked, tension filtering through her question. She leaned into him. "How can I do this thing?"

"Here's what I'm thinking…"

The Russians stepped forward and laid down fire. Once again the chambers of the subterranean paradise were filled with the alien cacophony of artillery.

The outer walls of the building were pelted by bullets. In answer, the men inside the structure opened up their own hornet's nest and let it loose on their foes below. Smoke from the gunfire began to choke the air.

Out from the filmy haze ran a solitary figure. Dressed in the black garments of a valleyman, it sprinted along, covering its head with a shawl of some kind and carrying itself with obvious timidity and fright.

"It's me! It's me!" yelled the figure, trying to raise its voice over the gunfire.

"It's Bring, you fools! Bring!"

The nearest gun emplacement to the man ceased firing, its operators confused. They heard insistent pounding on the door just outside the room they occupied on the ground floor of the building. They looked over at their valleymen counterparts.

"Open up! Open this door! They'll kill me! Get the Russian!"

The soldiers inside, bewildered not only by the appearance of the man, but by a string of unusual orders from their superior and the strange nature of the caverns, did nothing but stare. The valleymen, hearing the shouting, swiftly unbolted the portal and opened it.

The man outside rushed in and slammed the door shut behind him. Without hesitation he took to the stairs that ascended up to the next level of the building.

"This is insane!" the man shouted back at the valleymen. "Our home has been shattered. This is not what I wanted!"

Before anyone could question him, he was gone, though they could still hear him shouting. The dwellers below began to converse among themselves.

Captain Action readjusted the shawl that covered his head and looked around him. His hair had been quickly colored to resemble that of the valleymen. He had also used putty and paint that he carried in his belt for extreme quick-change emergencies to alter his face.

That, combined with some brief but crucial coaching from Uliana, made for a reasonable approximation of Bring, the leader of the opposition.

He hoped it would be the last masquerade he'd have to pull off for the mission; without plastiderm, he couldn't imagine his luck holding out much longer.

Pulling up before a closed door, Drake collected his thoughts and his nerve, then flung it open.

His eyes instantly met those of Flins. The lieutenant's head bolted upright from looking down at a crude map of the City that lay open on a table. Ringed around him was an assemblage of soldiers and valleymen. Bring, thankfully, was not among them.

"Russian!" the captain bleated, storming into the room. "I barely escaped! This is all gone wrong!"

He kept moving, trying to avoid allowing those in the room a good look at him.

"What is this?" Flins' face went deep red. "I thought you were going to fortify the…"

Drake realized the man was struggling with the language. He smiled to himself, happy to cause the lieutenant any small distress.

He got right up in his face.

"The jig's up, Lieutenant," he said in perfect Russian. "We're going to negotiate a cease-fire…*now*."

Captain Action flung off the shawl and tore away the rest of his disguise. He felt the collective shock leap throughout the room, from body to body.

Flins' eyes widened in horror and then anger; he reached for a pistol. Drake saw the move and lanced out with single, solid blow to the man's jaw.

"Back off!" he shouted. "I said I'm here to talk! We can do that, can't we? Like men?"

The Russian's inarticulate snarl of a reply made him seem more an animal cornered in the wild than an officer in the Red Army. Somehow, his men must have understood, for they pounced on Captain Action like ants on a lump of sugar.

Drake flung the first man off, but then went down under the assault of the next two. He lashed out like a hellcat, fists and feet flying, trying to stand again.

Flins quickly ducked out of the room.

Reaching the bottom floor by accessing a stairwell at the rear of the building, the lieutenant gathered up the remainder of his own soldiers and retreated out a back door. The portal emptied out into a small square.

Directing his men to the far side of the square, Flins caught glimpses of the City's inhabitants peering around corners and through the rare window that dotted the surrounding structures. He sneered at them and then ordered the soldiers into a tight formation, facing the building they'd just exited.

"Murom, bring out a mortar," he ordered. "Tambov, help him. Quickly!"

From out of a small alleyway that ran between two buildings, the soldiers fetched the equipment. Flins smiled at his cleverness of planting armament in the spot should they have to pull back from an overwhelming assault from the City's access tunnel.

Once the mortar had been swiftly assembled and positioned, the soldier named Murom turned to the officer.

"Sir, what do you intend?"

The lieutenant gazed at the man with disappointment on his face, as if it were quite obvious what needed to be done and the soldier was too dim-witted to see it.

"Blow it up, of course, Comrade."

Murom beetled his brow. "Blow what up, Sir?"

Flins turned to jab out with his finger, pointing across the square.

"That building, you brain-dead fool!"

At the tunnel's mouth, Juthrbog and Uliana watched as the return fire from the structure lessened and then died out all together. The albino wondered at that, unsure of what it meant.

Uliana roiled inside at her inability to know what was happening to Captain Action; it had seemed like ages since he gained access to the building. She trusted his abilities, but couldn't help but feel a cold compress of dread weighing down on her.

The sound of a small explosion echoed through the air. She could see no visible sign of it.

"From where?" she asked Juthrbog, scanning his face.

"From somewhere beyond the building, I…"

The lieutenant's speculation was drowned out by another explosion, this one from the upper floors of the structure they faced. The stone there burst apart, crumbled after a bright flash, then rained down on the street below. Another flash and another horrible explosion, this one lower on the building.

They watched in swift horror as the entire building lit up with fire and fury. The sound alone sickened them, but the sight of it was beyond reasoning.

Uliana Ulanova, the First Brighten, screamed.

Her home was under siege. The events that led up to the destruction before her were terrifying, of course, but the abomination that she stood and witnessed set her every synapse on fire. Her blood boiled in her veins, her eyes bulged. She could not see a path back from the moment before her. New Lake had been mortally wounded.

Juthrbog cursed his people, bitterly and stridently. If there had been a division between him and Flins and Marowit, it had now widened into a yawning chasm. He simply wanted to kill them with his own bare hands. This was not the way of the glorious Revolution. These were not the ideals of the state that he held dear. This was not the Motherland. This was evil for evil's sake.

Dr. Evil was gone, as Captain Action had told them, but surely and quite evidently his legacy continued unabated.

And, both the man and woman thought to themselves simultaneously, the captain himself was gone, too.

Perhaps their lack of faith in Captain Action could be forgiven, given the supreme stress of the situation. When the explosions had ceased and the sounds of pockets of fire came to their deadened ears, they saw a figure rise and run towards them. Smoke peeled away from the figure in wispy tendrils as it moved.

The Russian lieutenant caught the fleeing person and laid him down on the ground near the opening to the tunnel. His soldiers fanned out and covered the smoking, flaming rubble, watching for more attacks.

They unwrapped the shawl that wound around the figure. It was hot to the touch. Inside was Miles Drake, covered in soot and coughing.

"I'm okay, I'm okay," he insisted, sitting up and continuing to cough. "Gonna take more than that to finish me off."

He explained to them that he'd managed to free himself from the pile-up and rush after Flins. Seeing that the soldiers were exiting out into an exposed area, Drake spotted another exit and played it safe by utilizing it. The door took him to an alleyway, and before he could find his way out, the Russians began shelling the building.

He somehow managed to survive that terrible event.

The captain knew what the destruction would mean to Uliana, to her kinsmen. It would mean a crossroads. They would never feel secure again after that day. Not entirely.

Drake allowed the woman her space. He had done it before and he suspected he'd continue to do so. There was little he could say to lessen the impact of watching one's home destroyed piece by piece.

All he could do, he thought, was to continue forward, to rout the bad guys and help clean house.

Soon they began to pick through the remnants of the building, looking for survivors. Its devastation was complete; it resembled nothing more than a pile of smoldering stones. The faces of valleymen drifted up out of the shadows and smoke, a few brave souls who stared numbly at a sight they could barely comprehend.

"Captain, over here," came Juthrbog's voice from somewhere off to one side of Drake. He picked his way over the rubble to the Russian's side, then gazed down at where the man was pointing.

"What is that?" said the lieutenant.

In what looked like the remains of a cellar now choked with debris sat two large metal boxes. On one side of the boxes there were shutters, slatted panels that rested in open position. The shuttered sides of the boxes faced each other, roughly two feet apart.

A glow could be seen inside each box.

The captain suddenly felt someone tug at his arm. Uliana moved past him, almost pushing him aside.

"No, no, no," she muttered, her mouth hanging open in disbelief. The woman stopped at the edge of what was once the cellar's far wall and crouched down for a better view of the boxes.

"What?" asked Drake. "What the hell is it?"

"Damnation," she answered.

He stepped up to her, laid a hand on her shoulder. "Uliana, tell me what is it?"

She flung his hand away, then stood up and faced him with tear-filled, bloodshot eyes.

"Your doctor of evil, he will not rest. His abominations continue, though

"No, no, no," she muttered, her mouth hanging open in disbelief.

his brain lies crushed somewhere far below us."

Drake shook his head. "I don't understand."

"Look!" she screamed, pointing. "He has exposed the rock, the rock he was mining from the epicenter, to other elements! Uranium, I suspect, maybe others…"

Ideas came to the captain; horrible ideas.

"He was trying to, what? Recreate the original 1908 blast, perhaps?"

"More than that, I am sure! The sick, twisted *insanity* of it!"

"Wait," he said. "Why doesn't the mist, your miracle substance, take care of it? Stop the reaction?"

Uliana turned and spat at the rubble.

"Too late, too far gone. This is a reaction far beyond what the mist can handle. This could explode at any moment! I have no idea, no idea at all, Captain!"

He reached out to pull her back from the area, but she resisted. Finally, he lifted her up bodily and removed her from the edge of the cellar, away from the boxes. She punched at him, slapped him hard.

"What does it *matter*?" she screamed. "We are all dead!"

He set her down, then spun her around to face him.

"Because," he said to her quietly and firmly, "there are more of these boxes, if I know the doctor at all, and we need to find them.

"And then we're going to defuse them somehow."

XXIV

EXPULSION

"I don't like this," proclaimed Uliana. "I am not sure it is Truth."

"But it *is*," insisted Captain Action. "And it's the only path to get to it that I can see."

The A.C.T.I.O.N. agent had led them to the ruins of Dr. Evil's platform and rummaged through them, looking for something. Finally, he came back with an odd device in his hand, a look of grim satisfaction on his handsome face.

Then he asked Bury to assemble the valleymen who'd still been taken and been with the engineers when they were holed up in their huts.

Now, with the men in a line before him, the captain put the device, a metal skullcap with various protrusions, on his head and concentrated.

"What is this thing, again?"

"A 'thought sensor,' or at least that's what the doctor called it. If it still works I should be able to 'see' the location of the boxes in their minds," Captain Action pointed at the men.

"Uliana, listen, please – these men volunteered," he responded to her quiet fuming. "They won't be harmed. The doctor and the engineers did harm to them when they were under their collective thumb. Think of this as using one of his inventions for *good* rather than *evil*.

"And the clock's ticking. We don't have many options at this point."

The woman turned on her heel and marched out of the chamber. The captain forced himself back to his work. Soon he had his information. He profusely thanked the valleymen and told them they'd helped him strike a blow against Dr. Evil's invasion of their home.

He also declined to tell them about the boxes, not sure of their reactions.

"Seven!" he exclaimed, hurrying back to Uliana and Sean. "I should have known it! Seven boxes for seven engineers, each one of them responsible for their installation and implementation. I have the locations and there are only *five* we have to worry about."

"Five?" How's come?" asked Sean, confused.

"Only five engineers survived to activate their boxes," replied Drake.

"The other two weren't around to carry out the doctor's contingency plan, remember?

"Now we just have to figure out a way to shut 'em down."

He looked straight at the woman.

"Yes, yes," she said, arms folded and pacing back and forth. "I know what you are thinking, Captain. I will go. But I will need help to carry that much of the substance back with me."

Sean jumped up, excited. "I'll go! I can do it!"

Uliana frowned. "He *could* help," she said simply. "It would not be too dangerous."

"We're all in danger just being here," Drake noted, looking around at the ceiling to the chamber. He looked back at the two of them.

"Go. Do it. And hurry."

"What will *you* be doing?" she asked.

Captain Action placed his own hat back on his head and straightened his tunic.

"I'm going to give our friend the evil lieutenant one more chance to help us get out of here in one piece."

Unaware of the mounting pressure around him, the Sixty-Fifth Bury had failed once again to get his point across to the other man in the room.

"You shouldn't be here!" Bring snarled at Bury. "Things have changed! The old Truth is not the new Truth and you are not a part of it!"

"Truth doesn't change," Bury countered. "But foolish men do, unfortunately. You *must* reject this 'new Truth' and return to our ways."

The older valleyman could see the cracks in the façade of the younger man. He could see that Bring was at a cross-tunnel in his thoughts. But he couldn't press too hard at such a critical juncture.

"You condone the attacks by the Russians?" he asked quietly. "You approve of our kinsmen's violent acts against the outsiders?" He looked down at the belt of the young man and pointed. "And the use of our ceremonial knives to shed human blood?"

Bring looked up at him with fury.

"You don't *understand*! Before I was *nothing*. Now I am important! You have always had your knowledge and your position, but with my 'strange' thoughts of a bigger world I have always been a *freak*! No one else knows what I've had to endure! No one!"

Bury suddenly took him by the shoulders, stared deep into his eyes.

"Brighten knows. And you've persecuted her for it."

Bring's eyes widened with confusion. He opened his mouth to speak, but found no words.

"What is *he* doing here?"

The two men wheeled around to find Flins had entered the room, red-faced, angry, and shouting.

"Never mind," bellowed the Russian. "He is under arrest!"

Bury was not completely certain what the lieutenant had said in his language, but his intention was clear enough. The older man tensed, ready to bolt or to fight.

But Bring sprang across the room and in the blink of an eye had his sickle-blade at the lieutenant's twitching throat.

"This is my father," said the younger man, "and you will treat him with *respect.*"

At the edge of the shaft to the grotto below, Uliana checked that the large containers she and the young man carried on their belts and on their backs were secure.

"Are you ready, Sean?" she queried. "We must move swiftly, oh, so swiftly."

He reached out to take her hand in his. "Hey, don't worry; this is nothing. I've climbed in worse places than this. Let's get this gunk and get back."

He smiled and squeezed her hand. She herself managed a weak smile and squeezed back, then turned to lower herself into the shaft, setting her mind to the climb and pushing back the darker thoughts.

The darker thoughts that they might be too late. That her entire world might come crashing down around them at any second.

Planning out his strategy for attacking each placement of the irradiated boxes, Captain Action sprinted into the City. He oriented himself the best he could in the strange surroundings and then ran off towards a particular building.

He passed several of the City's inhabitants and called out to them in their language as he did.

"Seek shelter if you can! Leave the City! If you can't, get to a basement area or some other fortified place! Please believe me. You're all in danger!"

He hated risking a panic, but he could not live with himself if he said nothing to the valleymen. The boxes could explode at any moment, making all his words moot, but this was their home and they deserved to know that they were in mortal peril.

If only they had an idea of what time they had left, he thought, perhaps an evacuation could be executed.

He salved his soul by impressing the danger on as many of the City people he could. And he swore that he'd do everything within his power to try and halt its progress.

Drake looked up to see the towering building where his "trial" had taken place. Turning a corner to approach it, he suddenly saw Bury hurrying towards him.

He was accompanied by Bring.

The captain stopped, tried to assess the situation, make a plan of action to free his friend. Then Bury held up his hands in placating fashion.

"No, no!" he implored. "Miles, no! Bring is with us now! My son wants to help!"

Drake stared. "Your *son*? Okay, that's wonderful but I have something to tell you. Tell you both."

He sketched out the scenario with the boxes. Both valleymen were stricken by the horror of it. Then, when they had regained their wits, they asked what they could do.

"Hurry back to the Outer Chambers," said the captain, pushing them in that direction. "Uliana, Brighten, will be meeting us there. We think we have a solution.

"Go now. And if you have prayer or something similar, I'd use it now, if I were you."

"You're wasting your time, Captain," shouted Flins from a high window. "We're not leaving."

Drake could see that the Russian was ringed by his soldiers at the window, sharpshooters holding him in their crosshairs. He knew they could pick him off with one squeeze of the trigger, but he trusted that they knew and accepted the rules of parlay.

"Dammit, I've told you this entire place is going to explode any minute now! Get your men together and follow me out of here! We think we have a way to..."

The rock pavement at his feet cracked as a bullet slammed into it. The captain didn't flinch, just closed his eyes and counted to ten.

"A very good attempt, Captain," called Flins. "But a transparent one in the end. Bring all of your own people here and surrender to us now. I shall be lenient with your punishment. Then, perhaps, there may be some small place for you in our new party here."

Drake shook his head in cold realization.

"Then it's on your own head, lieutenant. Good luck."

And with that he sprang back, out of the line of fire, and was gone.

With several containers of the grotto substance sitting in front of him, Captain Action gathered together his team and gave them their marching orders.

"The boxes are here," he explained, pointing at five spots on a map of New Lake he'd cobbled together with help from Bury and Bring. It seemed that the valleymen had never had any use for such a thing, knowing exactly where they were at all times in their home.

Drake envied them that feeling of security and safe haven.

"Uliana has formed a thick draught of this substance," he indicated the container, "almost a syrup, that we will cover the irradiated rocks with. It should slow the explosive reaction and, hopefully, stop it all together.

"Then we can take the rocks and try to dispose of them somewhere else."

"There are several Deeps throughout our City," offered Bury. "Perhaps they can be put there?"

Captain Action nodded, comprehending. "Like bomb disposal chutes. It might work. Let's take care of the boxes first, see if this stuff will work."

"I will take this one," announced Uliana, stepping up and jabbing a finger at a point on the map. Her tone and her look allowed no room for argument.

"I will go with her," said Bring, holding his head up proudly. Uliana looked surprised, but simply nodded her agreement.

"Lieutenant," Drake said to Juthrbog, "you've got this one here." He indicated another spot. "Take with you whoever you want."

"My sergeant and I will go to this spot," said the albino, pointing to the map. Skrzak puffed up at the words of his superior. Drake thought the nervous little man had never looked so sure of himself.

"And I'll take the two that are left," the captain said. He looked up and across the line of eyes that bored into him throughout the chamber.

"I can move faster than any of you."

It was not said with arrogance or as a boast. It was a fact and the team accepted it after a moment.

"Go," said Drake. "And Godspeed."

Sean Barrett approached Drake after most of the others had left the chamber and rushed out on their missions.

"Cap, I can go with you, right?"

"Sean," the captain began, "I need something from the Streak. You know the signal beam projector in the equipment pack? I need you to get back up to the surface and get it for me, and the solar-energized power pack. It should be fully charged by now.

"Can you do that for me?"

The young man stood up straighter and saluted. "You mean it, Cap? Hell…err, I mean, heck, yes! I'll be back before you know it!"

Sean ran out of the chamber. Uliana turned to look at Drake, her brown eyes questioning.

"Will that help? These things?"

"No, but it puts him out of harm's way hopefully."

She rounded on him, her eyes blazing. "That was cruel. He *worships* you, wants to be like you. Wants to be *with* you, even in danger!"

The captain did not stop to face her, but gathered up his containers and flung them on his back, secured them there.

"Is this what you want right now, Uliana? To argue? I hate to tell you, but we don't have the time for it."

They'd been at arm's length from each other, or farther, since their fleeting moment of passion before, both of them with jumbled emotions for the other. In truth, neither one of them had much experience in whatever it was they were caught up in.

She reached out; spread one hand over his arm, feeling the tense knot of muscle there.

"Tell me what you are thinking," she asked him quietly.

Drake turned to face her, finally. His eyes roamed over face, as if memorizing it.

"I'm thinking about the two men, your two kinsmen, who came to America to kill me. They traveled so far for the whims of a madman.

"But they resisted the entire time. I saw it within them. That says something about the inner strength of your people."

He suddenly crushed her to him, holding her and breathing in the sweet scent from her golden hair.

"We'll get through this somehow," he said in the words of the valleymen.

"Your grasp of our language is very good," she told him, admiringly.

Drake's eyes twinkled. "It is also very *well*."

They moved in individual groups; the meshing of valleymen and out-siders fanned out and rushed towards their destinations with collective purpose, a shared mission. Everything now depended upon their speed and their determination.

Captain Action ran down the outer edge of the City, the containers slapping rhythmically on his back. Choosing the farther of his two destinations first, he scanned the area, looking for his target.

He pushed back the alien nature of his surroundings, the weirdness of his mission. It was simply people in danger, he told himself, no different than any other dire situation he'd witnessed before. Except, of course, the stakes were about as high as anything he'd ever known.

And, if they failed, the rest of the world might never even know of it.

Drake spotted the low, little building that sat apart from the rest of the city by about fifty yards or so. He ran up to it and looked for a door or entranceway. The structure appeared to be in disuse.

Finding a door on its far side, he kicked out at it, not stopping to see if it were locked or unlocked. The door splintered at his blow and he pushed it aside to enter the building.

In the darkness of the room beyond, Captain Action saw the glow from the boxes.

Without hesitation he ignored the feeling of dread that crawled up his spine and swung one of the containers from his back and uncorked it. Then he tore the metal box off its base and exposed the irradiated native rock that sat beneath it.

The container made a *glug-glug* sound as he emptied the substance from it and over the rock. The syrupy stuff flowed over the stone, covering it. To be certain, Drake uncorked another container and added its contents to the first.

The glow disappeared from sight almost immediately.

The captain then slammed the shutters closed on the other box. Stepping back, he stared at the native rock and watched. The glow did not return.

Feeling as if the substance were working as Uliana had supposed, he turned and exited the building. Once outside, he got his bearings and tore off running to his second destination.

He prayed that the others had made it to theirs.

The Russian Lieutenant known as Flins stepped out into his path.

Drake had taken what he hoped was a shortcut through the City to reach the other side and arrive near his second target. He had almost reached it when the Russian had appeared virtually out of nowhere to block his path.

The man was wearing a vest covered with explosives.

"Get the hell out of my way," snarled the captain, reaching for his sword. "You have *no* idea what you're doing, you idiot."

Flins unsheathed a sword of his own, a fine military blade that gleamed and glinted.

"I have every idea of what I'm doing, Comrade. I have done some thinking and have realized that you needed to be stopped in a more direct manner."

"There's no *time*!" Drake shouted, his face livid. "We have a chance to stop this city from blowing up all around us. Now get out of my way!"

The lieutenant took a step towards him, swishing the sword back and forth in front of himself, testing its heft and weight.

"Always you are rushing around, Captain. Always the man of action. Well, know this: if your doctor of evil truly could conceive of none other having this empire if he could not, well, I must admit that he and I are of like mind on that point.

"I would see it destroyed if I cannot rule it."

And he lunged at the captain.

Drake caught the sword thrust with his own and parried it. Then he jumped back, clearing a space between them.

"What?" asked Flins, smiling. "This old thing?" He held up his sword, turning it around, his eyes admiring every inch of it. "Amazing what the doctor had in his caches of weapons. I must commend him on his good taste.

"You, on the other hand, my colonel general called you 'Perun' after his mythological rival. But I think he gave you too much credit. I think…"

"*There's no time!*" bellowed Captain Action and moved in to attack.

Their swords connected time and time again, the clang and clash of metal on metal ringing through the City cavern. The captain discovered very quickly, to his disappointment, that they were too evenly matched.

While turning aside Flins' devastating sallies, he tried to orient himself as to where his second destination lay. Spotting it, he tangled his arm in the lieutenant's and then drove one knee into the man's thigh. Flin's leg crumpled and he went down.

Then the captain made a mad dash for his target.

He wasn't sure if it was the heat from his exertions in the sword fight or a phantom sense of an impending explosion, but his face dripped with heavy sweat as he slammed into the door.

The portal of the building in front of him cracked, but held. He threw himself at it again.

Finally, the door burst open and he almost fell to his knees when it did. Gathering his wits about him, Drake looked around, expecting to see the boxes.

The room before him was empty.

He spotted a doorway through which he could see stairs going downward.

Suddenly the room exploded around him.

Flins stepped over the prone form of Captain Action and looked down the steps and into darkness.

Glancing back at his fallen foe and then at the pommel of his sword, the Russian shrugged and moved down the stairs.

A glow at the bottom of the steps caught his attention. He flicked on a flashlight that he carried on his belt and swung its beam over two metal boxes. He could see the shutter arrangement on both.

Seconds later, Flins trudged back up the stairs, hugging the glowing native rock to his chest and grinning.

He passed by the downed form of the captain and kicked him savagely in the head as he did so.

"On to destiny, Comrade," he said as he exited the building.

"Let the Fates unwind their skein. They had not figured for Flins, the god of death."

Captain Action shook his head clear of the lights that danced within it. Feeling the immense lump on his skull, he shuffled to his feet and to the door, pulling his cap back onto his head.

Outside the building he saw the tableau, a frozen scene in three dimensions.

There was Juthrbog and the remainder of his loyal soldiers running towards the mouth of the tunnel out of the City. The lieutenant was yelling back at someone to follow him.

There was Bury and Bring and a group of their kinsmen on the edge of the city, near the ruins of the building that was destroyed. Their faces were etched with concern and confusion as they stood in place and looked around them at the evil that had befallen their home.

There was Uliana Ulanova, no, her name was *Brighten*. She was in mid-stride, turning her face from Juthrbog to see her captain appear in the doorway of the building. Her hair streamed back from her face, a golden blaze. Her lovely mouth was open, yelling something. Distress ran through her entire body.

And there was Flins, the god of death, with his suit of explosives, toting the irradiated stone of Dr. Evil. He was also moving towards the mouth of the large tunnel, behind Juthrbog and the other soldiers. The man looked calm, not crazed. He was smiling.

Reality rushed back in all at once with an almost audible crack of thunder. The captain moved into action.

He flew past Uliana and raised his lightning sword up over his head like Perun and then cocked his arm back to throw it. In a blur he released the sword and it flew directly at Flins, burying itself in his back.

Drake snarled, furious at his own actions. The man had left him no choice.

The Russian stumbled and fell near the entrance to the tunnel. His former officer and subordinates were already moving down the passage, well on their way.

The captain ran up to the fallen lieutenant. Within twenty feet he could see that Flins still clutched the glowing rock and was struggling to turn himself over.

"Stay still!" yelled Drake, but the man only looked at him and grinned.

He reached into his vest and extracted a detonator.

Miles Drake skidded to a halt.

"No! Dammit, man. Don't do it!"

"Death," hissed Flins and depressed the switch.

Captain Action flung himself away from the lieutenant, towards the mouth of the tunnel. He hit the floor of the chamber in a tumbling roll that carried him into the passageway.

The force of the explosion threw him even farther.

Drake ended up against the far wall of the tunnel, looking backwards. His brain struggled to comprehend what he saw.

The detonation seemed focused in a thick column of intense fire that rose up from the floor of the City cavern to its ceiling. Behind it, buildings on the edge of New Lake crumbled and fell from the shock wave.

Then the rest of the world fell in on itself.

Shattered, the stone and soil of the cavern's ceiling rained downward. In the back of his mind, in some small place there, Captain Action marveled at the combined properties of Flins' common explosives and the alien radiation.

Consciously, he watched in horror as the cavern began to collapse onto the outer edges of the glorious, medieval City.

Then someone was pulling on him, trying to lift him to his feet, shouting in his ear.

Drake was suddenly standing. But he couldn't stop looking back at the growing destruction.

Through the rain of debris, he saw valleymen running away from the fire and falling stones. He saw Bury and Bring, covering their heads and shouting, looking every which way.

He saw Brighten.

He thought he saw her look his way, but then she was gone.

The captain turned to Juthrbog and his soldiers.

"Go, go, go!" he shouted over the din of the cave-in.

They all ran one step ahead of the tunnel's collapse. They ran though they had no strength left to do so.

The rocks and stones fell behind them, nipping at their heels.

They ran out of the tunnel and into the Outer Chambers, then into the Gardens and to the Up, the way out of the subterranean world.

The sound of the collapse filled their hearing, threatened to burst their eardrums.

At the top of the Up, Captain Action spotted Sean Barrett. The young man was looking down at them in terror, shouting soundlessly.

Drake caught him around the midsection as he ran past and hauled him away.

They exited into a frigid world of falling snow.

Drake kept moving, holding Sean tightly. Finally he stopped, stumbled, and the two of them crashed to the ground.

They lay there, breathing heavily. After a long moment, the captain raised his head and looked around. All he could see was white.

He and Sean got to their feet. The young man was nodding at him, silently indicating that he was whole and unhurt. Drake reached out and pulled Sean to him, hugging him in relief.

Then they heard the sound of rifles cocking.

Captain Action looked up to see the Russian soldiers spread out in front of him in a loose formation, all of them pointing their rifles at him and Sean.

How quickly we slip back into our rigid roles in the real world, he thought to himself.

From out of the falling snow then stepped Juthrbog.

Drake studied the albino's face and saw the weariness in his pale eyes and the pain that hovered just behind them. With a sigh, he prepared to fight; he supposed the lieutenant might blame him for the loss of something precious.

They stared at each other, silently. The Russian held both hands to his sides and made a twirling motion with his hands. His men lowered their rifles then turned to walk away.

Juthrbog dipped his chin to the captain, curtly. His face retained its stony emptiness.

Then he too turned and disappeared into the falling snow.

After they found their parked vehicle, the captain made an air search over the area using a Directorate jetpack that he assembled from the Streak's trunk.

He flew up and over the entire length of where he estimated the City lay below the ground, several times until he expended all the fuel in the jetpack. He saw nothing of note. It was as if the City didn't exist at all.

Maybe it hadn't. Maybe it had all been a dream. Maybe that was the reasonable explanation for it all.

A lot of maybes, he thought, scanning the ground below him.

On his last pass, Drake finally spotted something that caught his attention. He landed and moved in to the spot.

There, in the deepening snow, he saw a set of footprints.

Crouching down to get a closer look, he found he could not determine how old they were, or who had made them. The prints were already partially obscured and distorted by the constant snowfall.

But they led away from the area. He saw no other tracks. Someone had left the area of the City and walked away from it.

His mind filled with many thoughts, Captain Action returned to a waiting Sean Barrett.

"Who were they?" asked the young man as they stowed away the pack and prepared to leave the area.

Drake raised an eyebrow at the question, thought it over.

"I'd say they were a strong tribe of people who came here a thousand or more years ago from one of the Northern countries, fleeing from a bad situation. Then they 'went to ground,' you could say."

Sean absorbed that silently.

"Cap, do you think," he said when they climbed into the vehicle's cockpit, "do you think that…"

"I don't know, Sean," said Captain Action, cutting him off gently. "I wish I knew, believe me."

He fired up the turbines and then swung the craft's nose around and engaged the thrusters.

"What I'd really like to know right now is exactly how you followed me all the way to Siberia."

Sean reddened, then a small smile appeared.

"Oh, *that*," he began. "That was nothin'. It was easier than that time I followed you to Australia…"

Some days it wasn't just that he wasn't himself, it was that he was too *much* himself. His real self, the one that felt too much, cared too much. Better perhaps to be Captain Action and whoever else it was demanded he be on any given day.

With the welcome distraction of Sean's voice, he reached out, pulled the mask down into place and headed for home.

THE END

ACTION MEMORIES

I have a confession to make: I almost prefer to write other people's characters than my own.

That makes me a heretic, a full-blown warlock, in some circles, I know, but it's true – give me an existing hero to put through his paces and I'm a happy little boy-writer. There's just something about crafting stories around pop culture icons that provides a certain thrill that, for me, makes all the difference in the world.

Take Captain Action, for example. The classic 1960s action figure that kids changed into heroes from comic books and newspaper strips looms large in my psyche – for reasons I'll get to later – and he stands tall alongside many other fictional characters in my personal bucket list of dream projects. Well, strike that. I've written him now, so I guess I can cross that one off the list...

Since the Ideal Toy Company's demise in the 1980s, the ownership of the good captain has bounced around a bit, but when "retropreneurs" Joe Ahearn and Ed Catto bought the property lock, stock and barrel in 2005, I felt that perhaps the character had finally found a good home. Thankfully, I was right; Captain Action's growth as a new/old pop culture icon over the last few years under Joe and Ed's guidance has been nothing short of amazing. And this novel is a result of that growth, if I may be so bold.

I'm proud to say mine was one of the hundred or so pitches that went into Joe and Ed when, in 2007, they threw open the doors of Action Mountain and asked for proposals for a new Captain Action comic book series. I didn't get the gig, obviously, but it was fun to try and reimagine the captain for a new millennium. Regardless, I became friends with Joe and Ed and continued to throw ideas their way. Fast forward to 2012...

Since I had begun to write pulp fiction, I told the guys that I thought it'd be cool if we did a Captain Action pulp story, apart from the comics. That idea rolled around for a while and then one day, out of the blue, Ed Catto sent me an email and said, "We're intrigued...tell us more." Tell them

185

more I did, and then contacted Ron Fortier and Rob Davis at Airship 27, fine purveyors of pulse-pounding pulp, and before you could say "Lester Dent," we had a deal in place that satisfied all parties. Captain Action would finally be making the leap from plastic paragon to pulp paladin.

I swiftly began to fashion an outline for the novel. Ed Catto suggested a Cold War theme, with lots of spy stuff and the like; I kept thinking how neat it would be if Cap went on the type of adventure that would make Doc Savage himself envious. In the end, we realized that the story could be big enough to encompass it all and by the time I was done setting it up, the Man of a Thousand Disguises would be heading into the deepest depths of the USSR and encounter a lost city…and a few ne'er-do-wells along the way.

The so-called Tunguska Event has been a popular focal point for many a fiction writer, myself included. I first learned of it in the pages of Gold Key's UFO FLYING SAUCERS #3, a 1972 comic that both thrilled and, frankly, chilled me. In a story called "The UFOs Arctic Assault," I witnessed that infamous 1908 blast over Siberia and a healthy dose of wild speculation on its origins. I was hooked. How could I *not* write something about it someday? It seemed like a great foundation on which to build the novel and from it sprang my lost city and a heap of trouble for Captain Action and company.

Joe and Ed also asked me to not be shy about using existing Captain Action equipment from the 1960s toyline as well as making up cool new stuff for the story. Not only wasn't I shy about it, I was downright eager to jump into it. You see, some writers supposedly feel hamstrung by having to cram toy tie-ins and whatnot into their licensed property stories, but not me – I saw it as a welcome challenge and a way to be able to better imagine the captain's adventures in my mind. Hey, maybe someday there will be some toys or collectibles based on the book's new characters and equipment – wouldn't that be awesome?

A Captain Action "bible" already existed, put in place to guide writers of the comic books, and I was urged by Ed and Joe to let it help me shape the characterizations of Cap, Sean Barrett and Dr. Evil. That also allowed me to concentrate on creating new characters to populate the captain's new pulp world, including a new *femme fatale* and a vicious viper's nest of villains.

Uliana Ulanova sprang almost fully-formed from my fevered brain, like Athena from Zeus's noggin back in Ancient Greece. Ed and Joe wanted to see a woman who could hold her own alongside Captain Action and be an all-together fascinating character on her own. On that score, I hope I succeeded. To my mind, she's something of a "Bond Girl," but also as intelligent and self-sufficient as she is lovely. I really hope you dig her, dear readers, because she's made quite an impression on me. And Captain Action, of course.

Having Dr. Evil rear his ugly head in the story was a given, naturally, but I also wanted to create some new bad guys – enter Veles and his lieutenants. The Russian setting led me to envision Russian soldiers and a dangerous scenario to vex Captain Action at every turn. The soldiers lent the tale its Cold War flavor and provided yet another type of villainy that could be different and distinct from that of Dr. Evil. And, being a fan of mythology, I thought naming them for ancient gods would give them a sense of power and presence that would lift them up from the level of ordinary villains. And Dr. Evil himself didn't suffer from neglect, oh no; he received a coterie of criminal cut-ups in the form of his dastardly "engineers," seven mysterious figures who I think could hold up an entire story all their own. Hmm, there's an idea…

By the way, I'm not exactly sure why, but throughout the writing of this novel, I kept hearing the unique voice of the legendary Bela Lugosi in my head as I wrote Dr. Evil's dialogue. Try it out yourself and see what you think.

Sean Barrett, our teenage wonder, is the character who, after the events of this novel, will become Action Boy, a companion action figure to Captain Action from the original 1960s toy line. Here, we find him before he's awarded the name and costume of Action Boy, but well on his way to becoming a hero himself. I tried to make sure Sean didn't suffer from "Wesley Crusher Syndrome," an annoying disease that too often runs rampant through pop culture, but it's you, dear readers, who will be the judge of whether or not I pulled that one off. I really like Sean, personally – hey, any plucky, scrappy kid who can secretly follow his mentor all the way to Siberia has to have *something* going for him, you must admit.

You may find this interesting, too: an entire alternate first chapter exists for this novel, involving Sean. I started it off coming at the story from a somewhat different direction, but soon realized that it was a false start; I quickly set it aside and began again, putting Cap right in the thick of it and moving on from there. My original first chapter was described in my outline, and Joe and Ed and Ron all suggested a different, more exciting route – and they were right. It was a great lesson for myself, and I think I grew as an author that day after I recognized that there was a better path to my objective.

Thereafter I fell into a solid writing rhythm and the chapters – and the action - began to flow. Much of my previous work has been short stories, but a novel is a different beastie altogether and I marveled at what I saw as the form's luxuries…and its pitfalls. I began to detail each chapter in a small notebook before I wrote it, hashing out the particulars of action and characterization and playing with beats and snatches of dialogue. Much of that dialogue actually came to me as I wrote at the keyboard, a practice I had previously adopted while working on comic scripts, to give it a sense of immediacy and, hopefully, naturalism.

Oh, the image on the front of that notebook? Batman. Why is that important to a Captain Action novel? Glad you asked.

Captain Action owes everything to Batman.

There, I said it.

It's true, you know; developed at the same time as the Caped Crusader's blockbuster 1960s TV series, the "Amazing 9-in-1 Super Hero" got the boost he needed from the show's instant popularity to be the hit toy of 1966. Stick that in your Action Cave and smoke it!

Okay, maybe I exaggerate just a tad, but to my way of thinking the fine folks at Ideal were sure lucky they'd chosen Batman to be part of their initial Captain Action costume offerings. That created a kind of symbiosis between the two properties, you see – in fact, TV's *Batman* and Cap lasted just about the same amount of time. By the end of 1968 they were both history.

But let's speak of happier things, like the wonderfully "fab" kookiness of Batman in Captain Action's world. That Batman outfit set, first issued in 1966, reflected the actual comic book hero about as much as the rest of Cap's costumes did – which is to say "close enough for jazz." The Caped Crusader probably fared a bit better than his fellow heroes as costumes for Captain Action; in retrospect; at least he's not carrying a gun.

I've often wondered what exactly the Ideal designers were smoking when they put together some of their toys. The Bat-essentials are all there: grey jumpsuit, blue boots, trunks, and cape, and the blue mask, of course. But why a blue utility belt? One assumes that DC gave the Ideal people some reference material – I mean, heck, there's a beautiful Murphy Anderson illustration of Batman right there on the box! And don't get me started on that cape! I'm warning you! I mean, *horizontal* stripes?

Still, in all, it's a really Zowie set, with an emphasis on BIFF! BAM! POW! I would have drooled over it at the toy store if I had been more than just a year old at the time. No, I first discovered Captain Action around 1973 and from an unlikely source: Stevie.

See, Stevie was this kid from Florida who visited these people – his grandparents - who lived a few houses down and across from my family on Parkwood Ave. All the way up from the swamps of the Sunshine State he lugged with him a strange Batman outfit, which I presumed to be a G.I. Joe accessory of which I was unaware. Maybe Florida had different toys than Ohio? Anyway, it was cool. Oh, how cool. Ridiculously cool.

Stevie was mostly a pain in the butt but he earned a few Cool Kid Points with that Batman gear. Surprisingly, he let me try it out on my own G.I. Joe and let me tell you, this fan of the 1960s Batman show was in Bat-heaven. Then the summer ended and Stevie went back to Florida…but he left something behind.

The day after he departed, I found the front piece of the Batman mask in the dirt outside his grandparents' house. And let's make something clear here; it was purely an accident. I was and remain an innocent kid. I held onto that piece of plastic for years, looking on it as a kind of talisman, an artifact, an oddity. What *was* it, really? Why did Stevie have a Batman toy that I, Master of All Toy Knowledge, didn't recognize?

If I squinted, it almost looked like Adam West.

I lost that piece of Bat-mask in the mists of time but never forgot it. When, at some later date, I learned all about Captain Action, it all made sense, but for a too-brief moment of childhood I felt as if I had found a piece of the Ark of the Covenant,…or a fourth season of *Batman*.

So, yeah, Batman kind of introduced Captain Action and all the wonderful heroes he could become to the world. And, in a way, he introduced him to me, too. Thanks, Cap.

While I'm at it, I want to thank Joe Ahearn and Ed Catto for all their belief in me and for their continued friendship, Ron Fortier for being the best gosh-darned editor a boy-writer could want, Rob Davis for his too-cool interior illustrations and fantastic design sense, Nick Runge for the cover that launched a million "wows," Joe Berenato for having my back once again, and, of course, The Little Woman for inspiration, consultation, and infinite amounts of patience.

And thank you, Stevie, wherever you are.

JIM BEARD (25 April 2012)

ABOUT OUR CREATORS

WRITER

JIM BEARD - A native Toledoan, was introduced to comic books at an early age by his father, who passed on to him a love for the medium and the pulp characters who preceded it. After decades of reading, collecting and dissecting comics, Jim became a published writer when he sold a story to DC Comics in 2002. Since that time he's written Star Wars and Ghostbusters comic stories and contributed articles and essays to several volumes of comic book history. Recently, he edited a book of essays on the 1966 Batman TV series, GOTHAM CITY 14 MILES. Check it out at www.facebook.com/gothamcity14miles.

Currently, Jim provides regular content for Marvel.com, the official Marvel Comics website, and is a regular columnist for Toledo Free Press. His pulp projects include his Sgt. Janus, Spirit-Breaker character, a Houdini adventure, a graphic novel adaptation of Manly Wade Wellman's Silver John for Sequential Pulp Comics/Dark Horse and a Richard Nixon pulp-style tale. He's also working on a Universal Monsters Chronology for Hasslein Books and a history of 1970s comics for TwoMorrows.

Jim's horribly un-updated blog is at www.jimbeard.blogspot.com, and he can usually be found hanging out on Facebook at www.facebook.com/thebeardjimbeard.

INTERIOR ILLUSTRATOR

ROB DAVIS –A native of Missouri, birthplace of Mark Twain and childhood home of Walt Disney, Rob was inspired by a Jack Kirby comic book at age eight (AVENGERS #2!) Rob has been drawing people and things ever since. Freelancing for Marvel, DC and Malibu in the 1990s Rob worked as a penciler and afterwards designing everything from T-shirts to New Pulp books. Rob has been nominated for the Pulp Factory Awards every year since its inception for his interior illustration work, and even won once! You can check out his blog and gallery at: robmdavis.com.

COVER PAINTER

NICK RUNGE is a professional painter and comic illustrator. His career began in 2004. Since then, he's done over 60 covers for titles like G.I. Joe, Terminator, Angel, Star Trek, Judge Dredd, Ghostbusters, and many more. In 2009, Nick penciled a Superman story for DC, and did Farscape covers for Boom!

2010 included Ghostbusters and Angel covers (#39-44). 2011 brought a Ghostbusters ongoing series from IDW, concept work for Hasbro and movie poster work for films.

Nick is now the complete art for an original graphic novel titled Fever Ridge, about WW2 New Guinea, to be released early next year.

He currently resides in Denver, CO
www.rungeart.blogspot.com
www.alamoscout6.deviantart.com
nickrunge@comcast.net
www.wix.com/nickrunge/nickrunge

Here's another book by the same author:

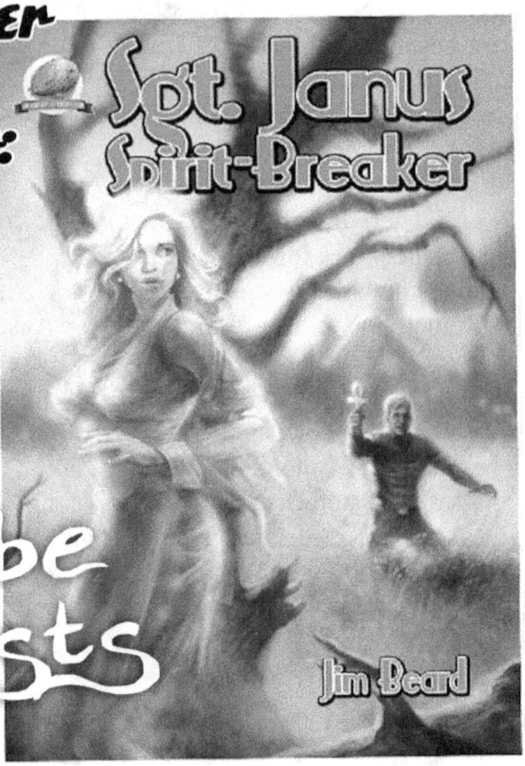

Sgt. Janus Spirit-Breaker

Here be Ghosts

Jim Beard

Situated in the rural back country of Edwardian England is an old, mysterious house whose unique owner earns his living as a Spirit-Breaker, a hunter of ghosts. A former military veteran, Sgt. Roman Janus has devoted his life to aid those haunted, both emotionally and physically by obsessive wraiths whose spirits are still anchored to our world.

Airship 27 Productions is thrilled to present *Sgt.Janus – Spirit Breaker* by Jim Beard. Part detective, part occultist, Janus is himself a man of mystery whose own past is shrouded and the motivations behind his calling kept hidden. Within this volume you will find eight tales as narrated by his clients, each with his or her own perspective on this uncanny hero and his amazing career. Filled with suspense, terror and agonizing pathos, each a solid mesmerizing journey into the unknown world beyond.

BLACK BAT MYSTERY

HE OWNS THE NIGHT

One of the most original heroes in all of pulpdom returns in four gun-blazing adventures cram packed with action and adventure. The mysterious *Black Bat* once again patrols the urban jungle, his targets, those who would prey on the weak the helpless. Crusading District Attorney, Anthony Quinn, was scarred and blinded by gangland hoods. When an experimental transplant operation returns his sight, it also grants him the ability to see in the dark! Allowing the public to continue believing he is a harmless, blind attorney, Quinn invents a new identity, that of the crime fighting avenger known as the *Black Bat!* With a trio of loyal aids, he launches his campaign against the forces of evil.

From a giant Nazi-bred monster to a gun-slinging Commie assassin, here are four brand new tales by Andrew Salmon, Aaron Smith, Mark Justice and Frank Schildiner starring the master of the night, the Black Bat, once again thrilling pulp fans with his daring exploits. Long considered the template from which dozen of comic book heroes were inspired, to include Marvel's *Daredevil* and DC's *Batman*, the *Black Bat* is truly one of the most unique characters ever born of the pulps.

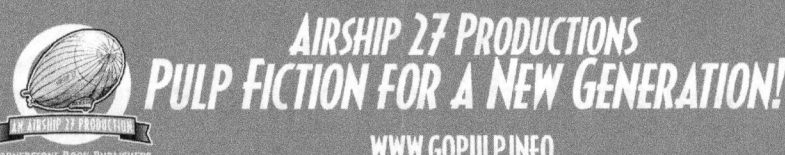

www.ingramcontent.com/pod-product-compliance
Lightning Source LLC
Chambersburg PA
CBHW071238250626
47163CB00001B/229